Practical Witches

A Practical Anthology of Magical Ladies

SUZAN HARDEN

This is a work of fiction. All characters, organizations and events in this anthology are products of the author's imagination and are not to be construed as real. Any resemblance to persons, living or dead, is entirely coincidental.

PRACTICAL WITCHES
ISBN: 978-1-938745-99-7
Copyright 2021 by Suzan Harden
All rights reserved

"Pig-Headed", ©2016 by Suzan Harden, first published
      in *Marion Zimmer Bradley's Sword and Sorceress 31*
"Cakes, Cookies, and Conjuring",
      ©2021 by Suzan Harden
"Knots", ©2018 by Suzan Harden,
      first published on www.suzanharden.com
"Love Train", ©2021 by Suzan Harden
"Unexpected", ©2017 by Suzan Harden, first published
      in *Marion Zimmer Bradley's Sword and Sorceress 32*

Published by Angry Sheep Publishing
Findlay, Ohio

Interior Design by JW Manus
Cover Design by Suzan Harden

More by Suzan Harden

Bloodlines
Blood Magick
Zombie Love
Zombie Confidential
Zombie Wedding
Amish, Vamps & Thieves
Blood Sacrifice
Love, War & a Bulldog
Zombie Goddess
Ravaged
Sacrificed
Reality Bites
Ghouls in the Grocery Store
Resurrected
Bloodlines Shorts Anthology
Bloodlines: The First Boxed Set

Seasons of Magick
Spring
Summer
Autumn
Winter
The Seasons of Magick Anthology

Justice
Sword and Sorceress 28
("Justice")
Sword and Sorceress 30
("Diplomacy in the Dark")
Justice: The Beginning
A Question of Balance
A Modicum of Truth
A Matter of Death
A Touch of Mother
A Twist of Love
A Virtue of Child
A Hand of Father
A Measure of Knowledge
(Coming Soon)

The Justice Thalia Stories
Snowfall
Murder Most Fowl
The Sweetest Poison

888-555-HERO
Hero De Facto
Hero Ad Hoc
Hero De Novo
A Very Hero Christmas
Hero De Jure
Hero In Camera
Hero Amicus Curiae
A Very Hero Wedding
Hero Ad Litem
(Coming Soon)

Solar System Services, Inc.
Alone Is Not Lonely

Millersburg Magick Mysteries
Spells and Sleuths
Fae and Felonies
Magick and Murder

Soccer Moms of the Apocalypse
Pestilence in Pumpkin Spice
(Coming Soon)
Famine In French Vanilla
War in White Chocolate
Death in Double Mocha

Miscellaneous
Sword and Sorceress 31
("Pig-Headed")
Sword and Sorceress 32
("Unexpected")
Practical Witches
Revenge Served Hot
The Yule Switch

For updates, news, and giveaways, join Suzan's mailing list or visit her website at www.suzanharden.com. You can also check her out on Twitter or Facebook.

Contents

Pig-Headed

"Change me back, Talis! I can't court Melinda like this!" Connor stared up at me, his little porcine eyes red with fury.

"And I told you not to interrupt me while I was practicing," I ground out through my clenched jaw. "Father told you not to interrupt me, too. The university examiner will be here this evening."

I wasn't sure what was worse. My anxiety over my entrance exam, or my brother wanting to marry my best friend. I tossed aside Mother's basic spell book. It had nothing on human transfiguration.

"Change me back, or so help me—"

"Shut up and let me concentrate." I rose and crossed the room to Mother's books lining the walls of her study. Goddess, how I missed her. Her encouragement. Her warmth.

The fact she would have kept Connor out of the study while I reviewed spells for my university entrance exam.

The rest of the village expected me to live up to her reputation as a sorceress. In addition to the everyday things she did like healing potions and predicting weather patterns, they claimed she had been responsible for warding our village against the ogre rumored to be living in the Viridian Forest to the north. Their expectations were so high everyone donated coin for my tuition in order to get a full sorceress back in our village sooner.

Though I did wonder how I would ever match her example if I couldn't master a basic transfiguration spell.

My anger back, I thumbed through one of the advanced books until I found the appropriate counterspell for humans. I closed my eyes and pictured in my mind Connor as he should look. Tall and broad-shouldered like Father. His blond, shaggy hair with the cowlick he could never tame. The twinkle in his brown eyes as he teased me unmercifully. I muttered the counter-spell.

Lady barked from underneath my study table, and my eyes popped open.

Connor hadn't transformed back. He still sat in the midst of his clothing on the floor, his tail straight and his wide ears flat against his skull. All the signs of a very upset pig.

On a positive note, I hadn't accidentally changed my dog into a human.

"Talis . . ." A low growl emerged from him. Lady

growled in return, and she inserted herself between me and Connor.

"It should have—" I turned back to the table and flipped through Mother's beginners textbook. Transfiguration of animals was one of the spells I would have to demonstrate to the examiner tonight. Transfiguration of a human should have been far beyond my meager skills. And yet . . .

My heart hammered and my head pounded as I re-read the instructions for the transfiguration spell for the third time. The blasted thing should never have worked on Connor to begin with!

"Talis!"

I pivoted on my chair to face him. "I can't concentrate with you shouting at me. Go sit in the yard until I figure out how to reverse this."

He huffed before he clambered to all four feet. His cloven hoofs tapped out his anger and fear on the hardwood as he marched out of the study and down the hall.

Once he was gone, Lady nosed my skirts. I petted her ebony-furred head as I poured through the pages. It was bad enough that I had a dog as my familiar instead of a cat. If I couldn't fix this, I could wave my admittance to the university goodbye. Using magic on another human without university accreditation was illegal. Even though turning Connor into a pig had been an accident, the king's court didn't have a sense of humor in these matters.

And if I wasn't here to protect the village, Goddess only knew when the university would assign a new sorcerer for the people.

By the time I discovered the proper method for restoring Connor, the angle of light in the study indicated it was well past mid-afternoon. I peered out the window, but there was no sign of a white pig lying in the front yard.

Damn, where did he wander off to?

I strode out of the study and headed for the front door, Lady trotting behind me. Too much of my precious study time had been lost, but I couldn't let the examiner see my brother in the form of a pig.

I yanked the handle and stepped outside. "Connor!"

Late afternoon light reflected off the sorcerer's globe in its holder next to the door frame. I could almost imagine it was lit. But it hadn't glowed since Mother's passing.

"Connor!" I yelled again.

A handful of birds sang in response. Dragonflies from the nearby mill pond buzzed in lazy circles around the reeds. Lady trotted past me and barked an echo to my call while she did her business.

Silence.

If Conner is deliberately hiding, I swear I will kick him in the seat of his pants.

Porcine grunts and squeals mixed with men's voices in the barn. My heart sank. Had Connor tattled on me before I could fix my accident?

"Come," I ordered Lady. She trotted back inside the house. I pointed at the floor. "Stay." She whined, but obeyed me as I stepped outside and closed the door.

I ran to the barn to find Father and Uncle Paddric separating the piglets from their mothers.

"I'm telling you, Andrew, all the grown ones are here and accounted for," Paddric yelled over the high-pitched shriek of the piglet he held. He marked it with berry ink and placed it in a separate pen with its litter-mates, also with bright purple streaks on their backs. As soon as he released the poor animal, it quieted and ran for the opposite fence.

"Well, then who does that white boar belong to?" Father asked.

My body shook, but Father needed to know the truth. "Are you talking about the pig that was sitting in our front yard?"

He smiled. "Needed a study break, Talis?" My words sunk in, and his smile faded. "What do you know about it?"

I couldn't meet his gaze. "The pig in the yard was Conner."

"Conner?" Even the other pigs, the normal pigs, quieted at his question.

"He came into the study while I was practicing a transfiguration spell on Lady, and . . ." My fingers twined and tightened until they went numb. I waited for Father's umbrage.

Instead, he and Paddric burst out laughing.

"No wonder he took off for the woods." Father roared even louder and clutched the side of the pen to remain upright.

"With Melinda chasing him all the way," Uncle Paddric wiped at the tears streaming down his face.

"Melinda?" I stared at my father and uncle.

"She brought dinner for us tonight. Between you studying and us preparing the piglets for the market, she knew we wouldn't have time to cook before the examiner arrived." He chuckled. "I think she simply wanted an excuse to spend time with Conner."

"I don't think chasing him through the woods was what she had in mind," Paddric said, which sent both men into another fit of laughter.

The woods. Goddess, what if there were *an ogre living in the Viridian Forest?*

I spun and ran for the stone fence marking our family farm. There was a horrendous ripping sound as I clambered over, but I couldn't worry about my skirts. Not now. I plunged past the raspberry bushes, adding more tears to my clothing, and raced into the woods.

Mother had taken me deep into the forest many times before she died, teaching me about the various trees, plants, and mushrooms. What you could eat. What had medicinal properties. What could kill.

She'd also taught me to identify spoor and tracks of various animals. Fortunately, the trail left by one frightened pig and one girl were easy to follow.

Until the growing gloom made the broken branches and scuffed loam difficult to see, and I had to walk slower in order to track them.

A burst of wind whistled by me. I stopped and stared at the tree tops. It didn't make sense. There was no sign of bad weather before I left our farm. If it rained now, I'd lose any sign of Connor and Melinda, but no downpour came.

I'd nearly given up on my search when I spotted the fire glimmering between the trees. I prayed the spell had worn off and either Connor, Melinda or both had resigned themselves to a night in the Viridian Forest rather than wander around lost.

But I spotted a huge figure moving around the flames, and I thanked the Goddess I hadn't shouted for Connor or Melinda. The form's head was too irregular, the body was too big, and there was far more hair for the figure to be human.

I eased closer. Melinda was trussed up and propped against a tree, her dark hair mussed and her blue eyes wide with fear. Connor, still a pig, lay next to her in a similar state. From the multitude of cords covering his snout, he'd tried to bite their captor.

The ogre itself whistled tunelessly while he whittled

a forked branch as big as my thigh. A second forked branch had already been planted in the dirt on the other side of the fire, and a much longer, thinner straight branch was propped against a log.

A spit.

My heart threatened to choke me in its desire to escape from my chest. All the stories and histories I read said ogres were slow-witted and slow-moving.

And they loved the taste of human flesh. Especially babies.

If I could untie Connor and Melinda, we could outrun it for home.

Assuming the three of us didn't get lost in the forest in the dark.

Well outside the circle of light cast by the flames, I circled toward my brother and my friend as another disturbing thought entered my mind. What if the ogre followed us back to the village?

No, we'd still be safe since the university examiner should be there by now, and he was a full sorcerer. However, if I brought an ogre back with me, I could say goodbye to any chance of attending the university.

I was so busy with my escape plan and my worries I didn't pay attention to the placement of my feet. My heel pressed down on a twig, and it broke with a very loud *CRACK!*

"Who there?" the ogre thundered. His voice was deep and gravelly.

I could run now and save myself, but there was

no way I could return with help before the ogre had cooked and eaten his prisoners. My only hope was either outwitting the ogre or convincing him Connor and Melinda weren't worth eating. Clenching my fists, I stepped into the little clearing.

"Greetings, sir ogre," I said. "Thank you for finding my friends and keeping them safe."

He grinned at the sight of me. "Good. More food. Mossrock hungry."

"I'm sure you're very hungry, Mossrock." I glanced down to my right. Both Connor and Melinda stared at me like I'd lost my mind.

Returning my attention to the ogre, I added, "My friends and I are much too old to be tender and delicious for you." To my recollection of Mother's records, no one in our village had gone missing in her lifetime, and certainly none had since her death two years ago. "How long have you been living in this forest, Mossrock?"

"Long time. Many seasons." After a brief pause, he added sadly, "Lost count."

"Has it been more than you have fingers and toes?"

His head dropped. "Don't know." He looked at me again. "Hungry."

He lumbered toward Melinda, and I stepped between them and held up my hand. "No, Mossrock. I won't let you eat them."

He stopped and pointed. "One is pig. Pig not human."

"The pig is my brother," I said. My admission seemed to confuse him. Before he could work anything out, I asked, "Who has been feeding you, Mossrock?"

"Sorceress," he muttered.

I took a step back. The only sorceress in leagues had been Mother. Was that how she really protected our village? By feeding the ogre?

"Sartra?" I squeaked.

"Sartra!" He danced. The noise of his stomping drowned my thoughts, and the ground beneath my feet trembled.

"She died, Mossrock," I shouted. He paused and stared at me. "She died," I repeated. "Two years ago. She was my mother."

He cocked his head. "Mother?"

"The one who gave birth to me?"

He nodded. "Mossrock had . . . mother. Long time ago." He looked at Connor again. "Hungry."

I actually felt sorry for the ogre. If he been dependent on Mother, Goddess only knew when he'd eaten last. Would he be hungry enough to make a deal? Or too hungry to listen? "I can feed you like Sartra did."

"You feed Mossrock?"

"Yes. I will bring you the best food."

"Babies. Human babies best," he rumbled.

"No human babies." I smiled at him. "But I can bring you a baby pig. If you let my friends go."

His eyes narrowed. "Why?"

Now, I was confused. "Why what?"

"Why let friends go? Humans lie." He pointed the forked stick he'd been whittling at me. The one big enough that if he ran me through, he'd kill me.

I lifted my chin. "Did Sartra lie to you?"

"No," he admitted.

"Then I won't either." I stepped past the forked branch and laid a hand on his arm.

And tried very, very hard not to make a face at his atrocious body odor.

"But if I don't take my friends home now, other humans will come. And they won't be willing to feed you. I will bring you a baby pig."

"Three," Mossrock rumbled.

I drop my hand from his arm. "Three?" I struggled to get my outrage under control. "Our deal was for one."

"Three humans go. Three baby pigs come."

It wasn't worth arguing with the ogre if it saved Conner and Melinda. "All right. I'll bring three pigs back tonight."

I reached for my knife and turned to cut the ropes binding Melinda.

"No!" the ogre shouted.

I jumped and whirled to face him, my arm outstretched and the knife quivering in my grip.

He pointed at Conner. "You do. Pig bitey."

I stifled a giggle. No sense in destroying the tentative truce. "You're right. That pig is bitey." I shifted to my brother and cut his bindings. "Don't say a word until we're well away from here," I whispered and waved my knife in front of his snout.

He said nothing, which was much more reassuring than anything else he could have done.

It was full dark when we left the ogre's fire. I led the former captives in the direction I'd come from, my knife still in one hand and the other supporting Melinda. Her legs were numb from being tied up for so long. However, Connor raced in circles around us and seemed to be fine.

Except for being in the wrong form.

I scored trees with my initial every fifty steps.

"What are you doing?" Melinda whispered.

"It's so I can find my way back to Mossrock." An odd sensation rose the hairs on my arms and the back of my neck.

As if we were being watched. But surely we would have heard the ogre if he followed us?

"Are you really bringing back three piglets to the ogre tonight?" Melinda kept her voice low.

"Yes."

"Why?" Fear tinged the single word.

"Because if I want any chance of getting my sorceress accreditation, I have to keep my promise. Our vows are their own form of magic."

"Talis! Melinda!"

Connor was far to our left, his white hide the only reason we could see him in the dark. "This way!"

"How do you know?" I demanded.

He snorted. "Because now that my nose is clear of ogre smell, I can pick up our scents."

"Maybe we could have him dig truffles for a season before you turn him back to human," Melinda said as we headed in Connor's direction.

"Don't even think about it," he retorted.

"I could do the counter-spell right now," I offered.

"No, I am not treading through this blasted forest barefoot! You can do it as soon as we return home." He trotted off, and we followed.

I turned to Melinda, who was walking on her own now. "When did you discover the pig was my brother?"

She giggled. "The moment he took off for the woods. He has that cute little quarter moon birthmark on his right buttock."

"Don't speak about my rear end!" he hollered over his shoulder.

Melinda's giggles turned into outright laughter. "And the more I called his name, the further and faster he ran into the forest."

"Hush, you two!" Connor halted and pivoted to face us. "Just hush! I'm the aggrieved party here! Neither of you got turned into a pig!"

"Then let's get home." All good humor fled from me. Would the examiner even still be there when we arrived? As long as I could return my brother to his rightful form and fulfill my bargain with Mossrock, I didn't care what punishment befell me.

As if to warn of my impending personal storm, a gust of wind rustled through the forest and sent leaves flying everywhere.

Connor's nose led us true. I wanted to cry when I saw the sorceress globe lit at our door. Did that mean the university examiner was still here? We trooped inside . . .

Only to find Mossrock sipping tea with Father and Uncle Paddric and petting my dog.

It was too much for me after the day I'd had. I stamped my foot. "What are you doing here? I said I'd bring three pigs to your fire tonight!"

Father folded his arms over his chest. "And just where were you planning to get these pigs, Talis?"

I needed to get Father and Paddric out of the house and warn everyone in the village. "Can we talk about this in the kitchen, Father?"

"No," he said sharply.

"I was going to buy them from you above market price," I said through gritted teeth. I didn't know what to do. Everyone I love would die because I couldn't master a stupid transfiguration spell.

"With what money?" Father insisted.

I was so tired, and nothing today had gone right, and I couldn't cry in front of an ogre because if I let him see any weakness, he'd lay waste to our village. "My savings for university. After what I accidentally did to Connor, and with the examiner not here . . ."

Except the sorceress globe out front was glowing.

I turned to Mossrock. I didn't light the globe, not even accidentally. He was the only new person in the house. Under the great-room lamps, he looked far more terrifying, yet far gentler, than he had in the forest. "You're not an ogre, are you?"

He set down his teacup. "Talis, I assure you I am an ogre." His voice didn't have quite the gravelly quality it had before. He smiled, showing green, crooked teeth. His clothes shifted from rags to proper university robes. "However, I am also your examiner."

Was it still the night before my examination? Was this simply a horrible dream because of my nerves? "I-I don't understand."

"An examination of a candidate isn't just about their potential skill. It's also about their character."

"Character?" I squeaked.

His smile faded. "The character test is different for every candidate. I arrived early, and your father told me what had happened with your brother. However, I had to discover if your brother's transformation was truly an accident, or if you'd deliberately performed illegal magic."

Connor trotted forward and peered up at the ogre. "It wasn't Talis's fault, Examiner Mossrock! I'm the one who interrupted her after both she and Father told me to stay out of the study. Talis worked all morning and most of the afternoon to reverse the spell, and—" His ears and tail drooped.

"You mean, until you foolishly ran away because you didn't want your lady love to see you as a pig," Mossrock chided. Father and Paddric smirked.

"Yes, sir," Connor mumbled.

The ogre turned to me. "It wasn't just confirming the accident. Talis, I was highly impressed with the curtesy and honesty you displayed while you bargained for your compatriots' freedom. Have you ever dealt with my kind before?"

"N-no, sir."

"So what prompted you to use that tactic?"

The truth may be ugly, but the examiner deserved an honest answer, even if he rejected my candidacy. "I originally was going to untie Connor and Melinda, and run away with them, but when I stepped on that dry stick—" I couldn't stop the tears welling in my eyes. "From the little I read about your people, I knew I could get away, but I was afraid by the time I got help, you may have done something horrible to them."

Mossrock nodded. "But something changed as we talked."

"I thought you were out there alone and starving." I sniffed. "M-my mother always said to treat everyone kindly until they give you a real reason not to. And if I could get food for you, then you wouldn't be starving, and you wouldn't eat people here in the village—"

I clapped my hands over my mouth at the realization of what I just said.

The ogre sadly shook his head. "There're many misconceptions amongst both our races about each other. Something we endeavor to correct at the university. However, I think you have already taken the first step."

He smiled again. "Well then, Talis, I trust you found the solution to your mistake. If you can restore your brother on the first try, we'll forgo the rest of your examination."

Thank you for adding more pressure on me. But I didn't say my impolite thought aloud. Instead, I recognized the second chance he gave me for what it was.

I recited the counter spell for restoring a human to their original form. Light flashed, and my brother stood on two legs.

In his very naked human shape.

Melinda nudged me in my ribs. "Told you. Quarter moon birth mark."

"Talis!" Connor shouted.

Paddric tossed a blanket at my brother. "Your sister wasn't the one prancing around our yard and the forest without any clothes."

Connor sputtered some more while he wrapped the blanket around his waist.

"Speaking of clothing," Father said. "Get some on before you come to the supper table. We have guests tonight."

"What about Talis!" my brother shouted.

I looked down. I'd forgotten about my torn skirt and the punctures to both it and my shirt from the raspberry brambles.

Mossrock rose, his bristly hair brushing the ceiling. "I can fix that." With a gesture and an incantation, light flashed over me. When it faded, my skirt and shirt looked almost new.

"What about me?" Connor said with an outraged expression.

"I cannot repair what doesn't exist," the examiner said innocently.

My brother stomped upstairs. A moment later, his bedroom door slammed.

Mossrock rose and extended his elbows to me and Melinda. "Ladies, shall we?"

We each took a proffered arm. This time, he smelled of crisp autumn leaves and river rocks.

"I hear you are quite the cook, Melinda," the examiner said as we headed for the kitchen. She blushed and murmured her thanks for the compliment.

He leaned over and whispered to me, "Back in the forest, I wasn't joking about being hungry. And I do love a good roast pork. Do you think your father would part with three of his piglets in lieu of a portion of your tuition?"

I grinned. "I'm sure he would, sir."

Cakes, Cookies and Conjuring

Tabitha Abbot placed a fresh tray of frosted tulip-shaped sugar cookies in the display case when the little silver bell on the street entrance door of The Enchanted Bakery rang merrily. Ozone from the spring thunderstorm followed Leslie Wilkinson inside and mixed with the vanilla and sugar in the air of the little shop. From behind the counter, Tabitha grinned as Leslie shook raindrops from her umbrella.

"I was beginning to think you forgot about Judge Reilly's retirement party this afternoon," Tabitha teased. Well, it wasn't true teasing. She feared Leslie would call and ask to have the cake delivered in the downpour.

"Nope." Leslie pushed back the hood of her raincoat to reveal her short gray hair with raspberry highlights. "More like we were swamped in the Clerk's Office."

"Something going on?" Tabitha asked as she retrieved the cake the courthouse staff had purchased for the party from the completed order shelf.

Leslie laughed. "Just the usual April rush between taxes due and fishing license applications."

Tabitha lifted the lid of the cake box so her customer and friend could examine the finished product. "This what you had in mind?"

It was a standard half sheet cake, but Everleigh had created a fondue sculpture of Judge Reilly fleeing his bench with his robes flying behind him.

"It's perfect!" Leslie looked up at Tabitha. "Honey, I don't know how you do it."

"It's the fairy in the back room." She winked, and Leslie laughed. It was amazing how much passed under the noses of mortals simply by telling them the truth. "Where did you park?"

Leslie exhaled wearily. "I walked."

Dang. Even though the courthouse was only three blocks away, chances were the box, and therefore the cake, would be ruined, if not by the spring storm, then by Leslie dropping them as she juggled the cake and her umbrella. Looked like she'd be making that delivery after all.

"I'll drive you and cake over to the courthouse. Let me tell Everleigh I'm stepping out for a moment." Tabitha charged through the swinging door to the back of the shop to retrieve her own yellow rain slicker.

Everleigh stood on a stepstool, the only way she could reach the counter designed for average humans. The fairy looked up from dabbing strawberry preserves in the middle of the peanut butter and jelly thumbprint cookies she was making. "You sure you want to be out in that storm. You might melt."

"I wouldn't be talking smack around so many steel implements," Tabitha shot back.

Everleigh sniffed. "I knew I should have taken that position at Keebler."

Tabitha normally took the fairy's sarcasm in stride, but that comment made her pause as she reached for her slicker. "You do know they don't really have elves working for them, don't you?"

Everleigh rolled her eyes. "You do know that was a joke, don't you?"

"Sometimes, I'm not sure with you." Tabitha shrugged on her raincoat. "And you do make mistakes. Like the rock band during last fall's Main Street Monster Mash?"

The fairy sniffed again. "That drummer shouldn't have been wearing those contacts to make his eyes look yellow. A real werewolf would have decimated this town within a week."

"You're damn lucky he thought you were high and didn't press assault charges," Tabitha retorted as she grabbed her purse. "I need to go out for a few minutes."

Luckily, Everleigh dropped the discussion, climbed down from her perch, and followed Tabitha to the front of the shop.

"Hi, Everleigh!" At least, Leslie knew better than to hug the diminutive woman.

The fairy planted her tiny fists on her equally tiny hips and glared up at the human. "If you wanted delivery, you could have just paid the delivery charge, you cheapskate."

"Everleigh!" Tabitha deliberately nudged the fairy's shoulder with her hip, hoping she'd take the hint.

The color in Leslie's cheeks nearly matched her highlights. "I was planning to walk back. I didn't ask for a ride. Tabitha offered."

"Uh-huh." Everleigh stalked around the counter and climbed up on the stool Tiffany kept there so the fairy could ring up transactions when she was out. Other than the dismissive noise, Everleigh seemed to drop the subject for now.

"Be right back." Car fob in her hand, Tabitha carefully picked up the cake.

Leslie held open the side door for her into the building's dividing hallway. The Enchanted Bakery took up one half of the first floor of what had been the downtown Apple's Department Store decades ago. Mama Jo's Yarn and Crafts took up the other half. The second floor was divided into one decent size two-bedroom apartment where Tabitha and Everleigh lived and two smaller apartments that were rented out to three graduate students from the University of Willowbrook who actually prized their quiet and solitude as they worked on their theses.

"I'm sorry about Everleigh," Tabitha murmured. "I don't know what's gotten into her lately."

Leslie snorted. "Honey, she's always like that." A

forlorn expression came over her face. "I really didn't mean for you to do this. My car broke down again."

Tiffany thumbed the fob to her little sedan parked in the back of the building in the lot reserved for the tenants. "You promised to get it into the shop. I told you my fix wouldn't keep the radiator going for long." Considering her temporary repair consisted of bubble-gum and a sticky spell, it was a wonder it lasted as long as it did.

"I know." Leslie grimaced. "How about we get in your car and you can lecture me on the way to the courthouse?"

The two women dashed through the rain to the car. Tabitha set the cake in the back seat before climbing in the driver's side. Leslie settled in the passenger seat and exhaled. Her breath steamed up the windows, so Tabitha pressed the ignition button and turned the defroster to full power.

"The real reason I accepted your offer for the ride is I didn't want to tell you this in front of Everleigh and get her upset." Leslie sighed again. "The county commissioners and city council sold the Falkland Building to Apollo Coffee and Tea."

A chill ran through Tabitha. "Why would they even want to touch the Falkland Building? The renovations would set them back more than a new building would cost. Not to mention, their CEO Lawrence Beaker considers Willowbrook too small of a market for one of their cafés."

"We're not that small," Leslie protested.

"That's what his press release said two years ago when Mayor West tried to woo Apollo to open here," Tabitha countered.

"But West is no longer the mayor, is he?" Leslie shrugged. "The renovations was the only way the commissioners and the council would agree to Apollo coming into our community, and Spartan Tires agreed to pony up some of the money for the restoration."

Double crap. The Falkland Building was directly across the street from The Enchanted Bakery. Tabitha depended on the morning donut runs from the local offices for a large chunk of her income. What would happen if the accountants and administrative assistants from the Spartan Tire corporate offices decided her little café wasn't worth crossing the street?

Tabitha swallowed her apprehension and tried to come up with a plan. "Do they have a projected opening date?"

"June 1st," Leslie said.

Triple crap. Tiffany gritted her teeth. She and Everleigh had less than six weeks to come up with a plan to save their business.

Later that evening, Tabitha was still chewing on the news while she made dinner.

"Did a grimchun crawl up your ass and eat your vocal cords?" Everleigh barked.

Tabitha jumped and droplets of marinara sauce splashed across the stove and wall. Everleigh gestured and mumbled under her breath. The faucet turned on and dampened the dishcloth, which then floated over to the stove and wiped up the sauce.

"What's a grimchun?" Tabitha asked as her friend magically cleaned tomato juice and onion off the wall.

"Nasty little bastards." Everleigh waved her hand in a pattern to rinse off the dishcloth and return it to its rack. "In Fey, they like to crawl into any orifice if you haven't warded your home or your campsite properly." She propped her fists on her hips. "What's wrong? You've been pensive since you returned from carting that cake to the courthouse for free."

Tabitha set the wooden spoon she'd been using to stir the sauce in the spoon rest. "You can't keep insulting people like you did with Leslie this morning. We're going to lose customers."

"Humans get off being treated like crap." Everleigh threw back her head and laughed. "It's the reason I tell you to be a little bitchier to your dates."

"This is serious." The initial anxiety Tabitha experienced in her car came back with the fury of a hurricane. "There's an Apollo Coffee and Tea shop moving into the Falkland Building across the street."

All the cocky attitude drained out of Everleigh.

"Well, that's just craptastic. Do you know what their record is for driving out small businesses?"

"Yes, I do." Tabitha threw her hands into the air. "Why do you think I'm worried?"

"Do you want to end our business partnership?" Everleigh asked in a very small voice.

"No! Of course not!" Tabitha stared at her friend. "How could you even think that?"

"I'm an outcast." Everleigh's face crumpled. "I think that every single day." Huge tears rolled down her cheeks.

Tabitha knelt and hugged the smaller woman. "You've been my best friend since I was five. I am not letting you go."

She had discovered Everleigh in her playhouse the summer before she started kindergarten. The fairy had been a literal bloody mess, her delicate wings ripped from her back as well as other assorted injuries. Tabitha had dragged her mother into the backyard and begged her to heal the fairy. Mom made a face and muttered it was against her better judgement. But they cared for Everleigh, and the fairy slowly recovered.

The night of the next full moon, the fairy tribe came for Everleigh. Mom argued they had cast her out according to their traditions and whatever happened to her after that was none of their business. A few spells convinced the tribe a witch wasn't someone to mess with, especially in her own back yard. Everleigh had stayed by Tabitha's side ever since, even through business and culinary school.

Everleigh drew back, sniffed, and scrubbed the wetness from her cheeks. "I can hex the construction crew—"

"No," Tabitha said sternly. "We are not harming anyone."

"If a nail gun malfunctions, OSHA will shut down the job site and investigate."

"No harm," Tabitha repeated. "Besides, we'd only be delaying the inevitable."

Everleigh scrunched her face. "If we want The Enchanted Bakery to survive, we need to come up with something that will knock the public's socks off their smelly human feet."

For the next five weeks, Mom and the cousins kept up with the regular baked goods while Tabitha and Everleigh experimented with various desserts. It needed to be portable. Not too heavy. Not too light. Satisfying. A blend of complimentary flavors, but in a new combination, something the people of a Midwestern town like Willowbrook would think of as exotic and fresh.

Each Friday afternoon, Tabitha walked down to the County Clerk's office with a tray of new desserts. Leslie didn't have to work hard to get her colleagues to evaluate the treats. They simply couldn't have one if they didn't fill out her anonymous questionnaires.

Unfortunately, the renovations across the street was a regular topic of conversation when customers came into The Enchanted Bakery. However, Everleigh made the effort to be super polite and pleasant to the clientele.

To the extent the new account manager at Corner National Bank asked her out, which she politely and graciously declined. Even Mom was amazed by the fairy's change in attitude.

Tabitha prayed her friend's efforts and their new recipes would help their shop survive the opening of the major chain. Each day that passed brought The Enchanted Bakery closer to the moment of truth.

On the Sunday night before Apollo Tea and Coffee's grand opening, Tabitha stood at the living room window and stared at the Falkland Building. With sunset, most of the businesses had closed, and the pedestrians had disappeared from the sidewalks. An occasional vehicle rolled down Main Street. Across the asphalt and concrete road, clean glass and brass fixtures twinkled beneath the antique-style street lights in anticipation of the brand new store's debut.

Everleigh joined her at the window. "I could still hex their water pipes."

"No," Tabitha said without taking her eyes from the potential death of her dream. "I'm not deliberately courting bad karma."

"Survival isn't courting bad karma," Everleigh

murmured. "And I've seen humans do worse things for lesser reasons. They don't seem to care about karma."

"But they don't have the power we do." Tabitha looked at her friend. Sometimes, she forgot how different Everleigh's culture was. "Would fairies hex each other in a similar situation?"

Everleigh gasped. "No! Never! I—" She sighed and leaned her elbows on the window sill. "I get your point. If we're going to pretend to be mortals, we win customers by being ourselves."

"That's how we have to do it," Tabitha affirmed. "For our own survival."

Monday morning's business was as slow as Tabitha and Everleigh feared. Across the street, people lined up for half a block. However, the few customers who came into The Enchanted Bakery raved about the samples of Everleigh's new apple and cheddar croissants. They sold a few dozen of the new baked good, but no one touched their usual doughnuts or muffins.

Everleigh brought out a tray of her dark chocolate and cinnamon cupcakes from the kitchen. She stared at the display case. "This isn't looking good."

"It's just the first day." Tabitha wiped down the back counter for the umpteenth time.

Everleigh slid the tray of cupcakes onto the top shelf of the display case before she propped her hands on her hips and looked up at Tabitha. "I'd believe you if this place didn't look like it was bleached within an inch of its life. You only clean like this when you're upset."

"You're not hexing anyone or anything." Tabitha glared back.

"Wasn't offering." Everleigh climbed up on her stool. "I'll watch the store while you go across the street and get us some coffee."

"Coffee?" Tabitha cocked her head. "Since when do you drink coffee?"

"Tall dark chocolate mocha, two shots of Valencia syrup, and whip, please." Everleigh folded her hands and rested them on the counter.

Tabitha pursed her lips before she said, "You want me to spy on them."

"No, I want coffee," Everleigh answered primly. "Why else did you stick a few bills in your pants' pocket?"

Tabitha shook her head. Of course, Everleigh had seen her slip her share of last week's tip jar in her khaki's. She reached behind her and untied her apron. "All right. I'll get you some coffee."

With the late spring sun shining overhead, Tabitha slipped on her sunglasses. Everleigh snorted behind Tabitha as she shoved open the street door, the silver bell jingling. It wasn't a disguise. She was protecting her eyes no matter what her partner thought.

She crossed at the street corner. The line for Apollo's was inside the new store this late in the morning. She pulled open the sparkling glass door and stepped into the cool interior.

The tables inside Apollo's were packed with customers. She waited patiently until she reached the section of the counter set aside for placing orders.

Unfortunately, Margo Wallace stood there, ringing up customers. "Why, Tabitha! So nice to see you! Checking out the competition!" She said it loud enough to attract the attention of everyone in the café.

Tabitha bit her bottom lip. The closest Margo ever came to being a businessperson was helping her mother run their family's beauty supply shop. Ever since Tabitha had challenged Margo for a seat on the Willowbrook Chamber of Commerce, the redhead seemed to have it out for her.

Now, she knew how the approval for Apollo's was passed, and why another corporation put up part of the money for the Falkland Building restoration. Margo's husband Robert was the CEO of Spartan Tires.

"No competition." Tabitha forced a smile. "We don't serve coffee, and Everleigh wanted to try some. Apollo's is supposed to be the best in the country."

"Everleigh's never had coffee before?" Margo scoffed. "What kind of American has never tried coffee?"

Tabitha shrugged. "I'm pretty sure she's had some before." She rattled off her partner's order.

"And you?" Margo smiled coyly with the marker in her hand.

"A tall cinnamon caramel macchiato." Tabitha

worked hard to keep a pleasant expression on her face and raised her own voice. "I think that will pair nicely with our new dark chocolate and cinnamon cupcakes."

Margo blinked at Tabitha's change of the game. "All right." She scribbled the order on the paper coffee cup.

Tabitha paid for the order and walked down to the pick-up area. The two baristas worked like the proverbial well-oiled machine, but the guy looked to be in his late thirties where the woman appeared to be in her early twenties at best.

The guy with Justin on his nametag winked as he slipped the protective sleeve on Everleigh's mocha. "Can I reserve one of those cupcakes?"

Tabitha grinned. "Sure." She lowered her voice. "But won't you get in trouble with Margo?"

Justin glanced at her before he turned back to Tabitha, all while working the espresso machine. "Don't worry," he murmured. "I've got dirt on her if she says anything." He shrugged as he topped her coffee with caramel drizzle. "However, I will bring a cinnamon caramel macchiato with me to test your theory."

Tabitha chuckled as she accepted the second cup from him. "Thanks. Your cupcake will be waiting."

He saluted before he turned to work on the next order.

"Enjoy your coffee, Tabitha," Margo's voice rang out.

Despite everything she'd told Everleigh over the last five and a half weeks, Margo's fake shrill cheer was the last straw. Tabitha looked over her shoulder and yelled, "Thanks!"

When she whirled around, she mumbled the hex under her breath as she pushed the door open to leave. The cash register squealed like a dying rat.

"Justin!" Margo shrieked. "Help me."

Tabitha glanced in the window. The register's tape dispenser was shooting paper all over the place, and the cash drawer open and closed like it was possessed.

Everleigh eyed her suspiciously when Tabitha returned with their coffees. "What did you do?"

"What are you talking about?" Tabitha handed the orange mocha to her partner.

"Between the canary-eating cat smile and the smell of magic, you're acting terribly suspicious." Everleigh slurped her drink.

"Margo Wallace is managing Apollo's."

Everleigh grinned. "What did you hex?"

"The register."

"It's Margo. She deserved it. Think of it as her karma coming home to roost."

Tabitha groaned. "I shouldn't have done that. The people working for her don't deserve me messing with their business. You know she'll take her bad mood out on them."

"She takes her bad mood out on everyone in Willowbrook." Everleigh slurped more coffee. "Just because her husband heads up the town's biggest employer, she thinks she's queen."

"I still shouldn't have—" Tabitha stared at the display case. "What happened to all the new cupcakes?"

"Sold them." Everleigh's eyes twinkled over the rim of her cup.

"All four dozen?"

"Yes." Everleigh grinned. "Don't worry. There's a batch cooling in the kitchen and another batch in the oven. And your cousin Lexie is mixing another batch as we speak. Before you say anything, they're already spoken for."

"Who?"

"Casa Tortilla didn't get their dessert shipment. Rosa was desperate."

"Wait! I need one cupcake for an order."

"One? Only one?"

Tabitha's cheeks heated at the flirtatious wink Justin the barista had given her and her promise to him. "Just one."

Everleigh rolled her eyes. "Then I'd better finish my coffee and get back to the kitchen. Rosa's expecting the next batch before the dinner rush. I already told her we'd have to substitute some Heaven Sent and Angel and Devil cupcakes."

The second Everleigh disappeared into the kitchen, the lunch crowd started trickling into the shop. Apparently, the dark chocolate cinnamon cupcakes were a hit at Casa Tortilla, and the staff told their customers the source. The clientele were disappointed they were out of the specialty cupcakes, but they were willing to buy cookies, scones, and other flavors of cupcakes.

Surprisingly, the flow of customers didn't slow down. The news of Everleigh's latest concoction was spreading through town like crazy. Tabitha had orders well into the fall.

Rosa's son Al showed up at three in the afternoon to collect the Mexican restaurant's order. He said their phone had been ringing off the hook with requests and, in some cases, demands for the new cupcakes.

Everything sold out by the time closing time rolled around. Tabitha followed the last customer to the door, but before she could turn the sign and lock the door, Justin's pleading face appeared in the window. She opened the door once again and made a point of flipping the sign to CLOSED.

"Come in." She gestured for him to enter. "Quick before someone sees you."

"Like Margo?" He chuckled. An Apollo coffee cup was firmly grasped in his hand.

"If only it were that simple." Her phone beeped, and she checked it. Another order for the chocolate cinnamon cupcakes. "I didn't expect our new recipe to explode like it did." She slid her phone into her pocket and faced Justin again. "Give me a sec. I did manage to save one for you like I promised."

Tabitha ran to the kitchen and retrieved the white

single-item box she'd set aside for him. Thankfully, Everleigh had gone upstairs to nap for a couple of hours. They'd be up late, getting a head start on tomorrow's orders.

When Tabitha returned to the front room with a napkin and a fork, Justin sat at the closer of the two small tables for customers. She handed him the box and utensils.

"Why don't you join me?" He waved at the other chair.

"All right." She grabbed a bottle of water form the soft drink cooler and sat down across from him.

"Do you want a bite?" He opened the box and pushed it to the center of the table.

"Goddess, no!" She laughed. "I have to run a couple of miles every day to keep my taste testing off my butt."

Justin cut into the rich cake piled high with mocha cinnamon frosting. He chewed the bite with a thoughtful expression, like he was analyzing the flavors. He swallowed and sipped his coffee.

"You're right." He nodded. "That does pare well with our cinnamon caramel macchiato." He set the fork in the box and looked her in the eye. "How much for the recipes?"

"Excuse me?" Tabitha leaned away from the table.

"How much for the cupcake and frosting recipes?" Like restating the question would make a difference.

"I'm sorry." She crossed her arms. "Our recipes are not for sale."

He pulled a checkbook from his back pocket. "I'm serious. Name your figure. I already know you supply this dessert to a local restaurant."

She cocked her head. "Why on earth would a barista think he could buy our hard work?"

"Because I'm a barista who is a silent partner in Apollo's Coffee and Tea."

"What?" Her mouth was hanging open, but she couldn't seem to close it. "Who are you?"

"Justin Beaker. My cousin is the face and money man. I do product selection and store openings." He shrugged. "I'm trying to get Larry to help smaller towns."

"How?" she demanded.

"Renovate historic sites like the Falkland Building." He waved in the general direction of Apollo's. "Resuscitate small town Main Streets. Create more jobs than just service industry positions."

"That's very noble." She shook her head. "But I'm not interested in selling any of our recipes."

Justin moved the fork so it fit inside the box and closed the lid. "Think about my offer. And let me know what your business partner says." He stood, laid a hundred-dollar bill on the table, and placed his checkbook into his back pocket. "Your cupcakes are delicious, Ms. Abbot."

With that, he picked up the box with the remnants of his cupcake and left the shop. The silver bell tingled dully behind him.

Tabitha unfolded her tight arm muscles, forced herself to her feet, and strode over to lock the doors.

When Everleigh woke up, Tabitha relayed Justin's offer. The fairy whistled and started pacing in their living room. "So Apollo CEO Lawrence Beaker sends his cousin Justin to be his hatchet man."

"Well?" Tabitha asked after Everleigh's fifth trip across the rug.

The fairy propped her fists on her hips and cocked her head. "Our recipes are our business. Do you want to accept his offer?"

"Hell, no! I hate that he thought he could just buy me." Tabitha sucked in a deep breath. "Do you want to sell the business?"

"No. Can I hex him now?"

Tabitha laughed. "Not him. At least, not directly."

Everleigh's eyes narrowed. "So what's your plan?"

"Rosa gave me a good idea. We supply desserts to every other restaurant in town."

On Tuesday morning, Operation Spread the Wealth was launched. It turned out The Enchanted Bakery wasn't the only business Justin tried flirt his way into or cause problems with.

Rachel at Night Club Café said Justin had tried to convince her to come manage the new Apollo's. She laughed in his face, and suddenly, she had problems with her suppliers. She grabbed onto Tabitha's offer of a deal to carry liquor-flavored brownies during her Friday and Saturday open mike nights.

Rosa got exclusive rights to carry the dark chocolate cinnamon cupcakes at Casa Tortilla which they served with a scoop of River City's Vanilla Bean ice cream.

Harold at River City Ice Cream and Fine Chocolates wanted something to go with their seasonal peach ice cream. Everleigh came up with a pecan cupcake with bourbon and brown sugar frosting.

For Wong's Garden, Tabitha developed an almond cupcake with egg white frosting. In return, the Wongs let her carry the oolong tea they imported directly from China.

When Tabitha told Mom what she and Everleigh were up against, all the Abbot women in the county showed up at the bakery's back door. They had the kitchen running twenty-four hours a day.

Over the course of June, customers were still going to Apollo's for morning coffee, but no one was eating there. Everleigh finally admitted she magically amplified the taste of the preservatives in Apollo's prepackaged food.

Near the end of the business day on July 1st, the silver bell jangled on The Enchanted Bakery's street door. Tabitha looked up to find Justin entering. He crossed to the counter. Thankfully, all she had left in the display case were oatmeal raisin cookies.

"A simple no to my offer would have sufficed, Ms. Abbot," he said.

"Does this mean you're not going to flirt your way into my business again?" she asked, affecting an innocent air.

"Is that why you turned the entire town against me?" He frowned and crossed his arms. "Because you think I was flirting with you?"

"No, you made me realize my business wasn't fulfilling its potential." She matched his stance.

"What does your partner think about this?"

The kitchen door banged open, and Everleigh marched into the public area of the shop. "She thinks you approached the average-sized partner and ignored the little partner."

"Excuse me?" Justin dropped his arms and stared at her.

Everleigh propped her fists on her hips. "You heard me. There's even laws about treating me differently because I'm shorter than Tabitha. We both know why you approached her first. Same reason you tried to woo Rachel down at Night Club Café. Well, you can just stick it—"

"He got your point." Tabitha returned her attention to Justin. "And we didn't have to do a damn thing. You said you were trying to convince your cousin to invest in small towns. But between you and Margo, you've already shown that's not the case."

"All right." Justin eyed Everleigh. "I'm making this offer directly to you both so there's no misunderstanding. What would it take to buy out The Enchanted Bakery?"

"You really don't get it." Tabitha shook her head. "To you, this is just something you can throw money at. To us, this is our home. Our livelihood."

"Margo is right about you." He turned to leave.

As much as Tabitha wanted to ask him what he meant, to do so would have shown she cared. Besides, Goddess only knew what kind of crap Margo had made up. The silver bell jangled angrily as he jerked the door open and stomped outside.

"Tabitha?"

She turned to find Mom standing in the kitchen doorway. "Yes?"

"That boy has some bad karma coming his way."

"But you always told me not to court bad karma myself."

"I agree with your mother." Everleigh's shoulders were tense as she stared out the window at Justin's receding back. He jaywalked across Main Street to the tune of several cars honking at him.

"I don't want a war," Tabitha murmured.

"You've already got one," Mom said. "You'd better fight to win it."

The next morning, Tabitha discovered Justin believed the same as Mom. A rat sat in the display case
and munched on the oatmeal and raisin cookies she'd
forgotten to remove. Instead of running, the rodent
spoke to Everleigh.

"A human male with light skin and dark hair
dropped him down the ventilation shaft from the roof,"
she translated angrily. "Black Claw apologizes for eating our cookies, but the human hadn't fed him for the
past three days, and he was really hungry."

"Is he all right?" Tabitha asked. Dang, Mom wasn't
joking about Justin. He could have killed the poor rat
with the two-story fall.

"He says he is except for some bumps and bruises."
Everleigh stroked his fur, but she had the faraway look
she got when she used her Second Sight. "No broken
bones or internal injuries."

The store phone started ringing, and Tabitha picked
up the receiver. "The Enchanted Bakery."

"Uh, hi, Tabby," Kate McKenzie said. "Look, I hate
calling you this early—"

Tabitha's stomach turned upside down. "Are you at
the *Daily News*?"

The editor hesitated before she said, "Yeah. Look, we
received a picture from an unknown e-mail account. It
appears to be taken through your store window, and it

shows a rat sitting in your display case. I'm having it checked to see if it was altered—"

"Don't bother," Tabitha said angrily. "Everleigh's pet rat escaped from its cage. I'm sure someone spotted him from the sidewalk. Don't worry. I'm sanitizing the heck out of the bakery, and you can quote me on that. You also can add in your online article we'll be late opening this morning."

Kate hesitated before she said, "You sure about that, Tabby?"

"I've got nothing to hide." She carefully replaced the receiver when she really wanted to slam it. She and Everleigh exchanged looks.

"I could hex their coffee—" the fairy began while she stroked the rat's fur.

"No, we're not hurting innocent people."

"What about their espresso machines?"

Tabitha shook her head. "The kids working there don't deserve to be injured or maimed either." She cocked her head and regarded the rat. "Would your friend be interested in some revenge against the human who starved him?"

Everleigh and Black Claw squeaked back and forth a few times before the fairy grinned up at Tabitha. "He's in, and he thinks his family would help."

As soon as the *Daily News*'s online edition went live, the phone started ringing off the hook. A lot of people called to support Tabitha and Everleigh, but a few were downright nasty. It was also no surprise when the county health inspector showed up on their doorstep at noon.

"That didn't look like no durn pet rat in the picture," he grumbled from beneath his huge moustache.

"You're more than welcome to check Black Claw's cage in our apartment upstairs," Tabitha said. "We've owned this shop ten years, and it's the first time one of her pets has ever escaped."

"You've had rats here for the last ten years?" The bushy eyebrows that matched his moustache climbed his forehead.

"Only upstairs in the apartment," Everleigh asserted. "Never in the shop until Blackie escaped. He's a smart one."

"And we totally sanitized the shop," Tabitha said for the umpteenth time that day.

"I still have to check everything," The inspector said.

Three hours later, he'd checked every nook and cranny of The Enchanted Bakery. When he didn't find so much as a dead fly in the store, he followed Everleigh up to the apartment. Thankfully, she convinced Black

Claw the ruse was necessary. He agreed to the cage in return for an extra dozen oatmeal cookies.

In the end, the inspector did write them up for allowing a domestic animal in the store. It was a minor infraction and a much lower fine than a pest problem.

Once they closed the shop for the day, they released Black Claw from his cage. He squeaked to Everleigh, and she answered in kind.

"Is there a problem?" Tabitha asked.

"No, he's merely confirming our offer." The fairy smiled. "Can you drive him to Riverside Park so no one sees him?"

"No problem."

Everleigh had Black Claw climb into a mesh shopping bag.

Tabitha headed downstairs with the bag, her purse, and her car fob. She stepped through the back door to find Margo standing by her car. Under her breath, Tabitha muttered a glamour spell to make the mesh beg appear empty. Margo didn't appear to notice Black Claw.

"Why are you skulking back here?" Tabitha demanded.

"I-I—" Margo fidgeted. "I didn't think he'd deliberately sabotage your bakery."

"Who?" Tabitha suspected, but she wanted to hear it from the source.

"J-Justin." Margo gulped. "Justin Beaker."

"What do you mean about him sabotaging the bakery?" Tabitha demanded.

"H-he took the picture of the rat inside your shop." Margo appeared to be on the edge of tears. "I think he put it inside somehow."

Tabitha cocked her head. "Why are you telling me this now?"

"I thought bringing in a major chain like Apollo's would help Willowbrook." Margo hugged herself and could no longer meet Tabitha's gaze. "But h-he's . . ."

"He thinks he can buy anyone," Tabitha said.

Margo nodded and sniffed loudly. "Is this what I look like to everyone in town?"

Maybe she was having a breakthrough in self-awareness. As much as Tabitha wanted to yell at Margo, she couldn't.

"We've had differences of opinion, Margo, but I've never seen you deliberately try to damage someone's livelihood."

"I-I just wanted to learn from him." Margo swiped at her cheeks. "My parents and my husband think I'm an idiot. All I wanted from them was some seed money to build something of my own."

Tabitha blew out a deep breath. She understood the need of making something that was yours alone, but her family had always backed her dreams. "Margo, thank you for telling me. You can quit your job as manager, you know. You don't have to follow Justin's path."

"But if I do, my parents and Robert will make fun of me." Margo raised her head. Fat tears rolled down her face.

"Not if you tell them the truth," Tabitha said softly. "Go home. Call in sick tomorrow if you need more time to think. Thank you for talking to me."

Margo nodded and walked down the alley in the direction of the library.

Tabitha looked down at Black Claw. "If I had any doubts about our plan, they're over now."

At seven-forty-five the next morning, Black Claw and his relatives upheld their part of the bargain Everleigh had struck. Screams drew the fairy and Tabitha's family from the kitchen.

They all stood at the window and watched patrons chased out of Apollo's Tea and Coffee Café by thousands of rats. Some folks climbed on the wrought-iron tables and chairs on the sidewalk and danced in fear. Others raced in all direction, literally bringing car traffic on Main Street to a screeching halt.

Everleigh climbed up on her stool and dialed three digits on the antique rotary phone. "Hey, Meg! It's Everleigh at The Enchanted Bakery. There's something weird going on over at Apollo's." She paused. "Yep, people running all over the place and a zillion rats pouring out of the café." Another pause. "Awww, thanks. I'll make sure to save a dark chocolate cinnamon cupcake for you."

She hung up, climbed down from the stool, and crossed back to the window. "Meg's got 9-1-1 calls coming in like crazy."

"It's good people are watching out for each other," Tabitha commented.

Outside, Leslie Wilkinson and three of her staff from the County Clerk's office raced across the street, making a beeline for The Enchanted Bakery. Honking filled the air, and the rats were starting their escape now that their work was done.

"Mom, would you start another pot of black tea?" Tabitha asked. "I think we're going to need it."

Mom and the cousins all headed back for the kitchen, chuckling amongst themselves.

"Would you double the order of oats?" Everleigh looked up at Tabitha. "Those rats earned their cookies."

Video of the rat invasion at Apollo's went viral and even appeared on the national evening news. Justin Beaker was last seen slinking aboard a jet in Toledo. Lawrence Beaker issued a statement that opening a café in Willowbrook had been a mistake, one he would thoroughly investigate.

Four weeks after the Great Rat Invasion, Margo

strode into The Enchanted Bakery with a bright smile on her face.

"What can I do for you?" Tabitha asked.

"I need a dozen assorted doughnuts, but I'm really here for a business proposal."

"Oh." Tabitha raised an eyebrow while she filled the white cardboard box. "What kind of proposal?"

"My parents are buying the Falkland Building." Excitement danced in Margo's eyes. "Lawrence Beaker is selling it for a song after the vermin incident. The doughnuts are for staff at the title company." She took a deep breath and released it. "I going to open a pub in the old Apollo Café. Mom and Dad are letting me lease-to-buy the building."

"A pub? That's great." Tabitha closed and sealed the box.

"And I was hoping you and Everleigh might be willing to develop three new desserts exclusive to my pub like you have for some of the other restaurants." Margo had a sheepish expression. "That was one of my parents' conditions for the pub."

Everleigh came out of the kitchen with a tray of lemon lavender cookies. "Try one of these and see if it fits your requirements."

Margo picked a cookie off the tray and took a bite. "Umm!" Her eyes widened. "These are wonderful." A concerned look crossed her face. "I don't suppose you could do a cake version of these cookies?"

"I'll get to work on it plus some other selections for you to choose from." Everleigh smiled brightly.

"Here's a down payment for the research and development." Margo pulled an envelope out of her shoulder bag along with bills to pay for the doughnuts. "Let me know when you're ready for a taste-testing. And would you walk the contract over to me across the street when you have the chance?" If anything, Margo's expression grew more sheepish. "I'll be over there, helping with the remodeling. I'm actually looking forward to getting my hands dirty."

"Sure thing." Tiffany said.

Margo popped the rest of the cookie in her mouth before she shook Tabitha's and Everleigh's hands in turn. "See you later!" She took the box of doughnuts and strode out of the bakery.

Everleigh placed the tray in the empty section of the display case and wiped her hands on her apron. "Karma?"

"Karma." Tabitha nodded.

"I still don't get some human behavior, but I'll concede your point about actions and reactions." Everleigh started back toward the kitchen, but she pivoted to face Tabitha again. "Speaking of karma, we're going to need to hire more people if we supply another restaurant. Even with your family working here, our combined talents aren't going to keep up."

"I know."

"No mortals," Everleigh added.

"I know." Tabitha grinned. "I'll have Mom put out feelers through the coven grapevine."

The fairy exited to the kitchen, and Tabitha opened the envelope. There were enough zeros on the check to make any deal with Margo worthwhile.

Yes, this was why she paid attention to karma. You never knew when the wheel would come around for you.

Knots

I handed Grandma the hank of black and white yarn twisted into a series of complicated knots. Balancing on the rickety chair, she hung her construction above the kitchen door. Cheerful light from the lamp hanging over the table winked against the copper bracelet she wore for her arthritis, the glow a sharp contrast against the inky sky visible through the closed screen door. The night wasn't silent though. A dog's bark ricocheted between mountain pines, and crickets sang their bedtime song.

She climbed down, brushed her hands against her polyester slacks and smiled at me. "All done."

Mama snorted into her glass of whiskey before she took another sip. She'd been working on the bottle all night, a common occurrence since Grandpa died last year.

The look Grandma shot her was the same one she would have given me before taking a switch to my backside for the worst of my sins. No switch was in

Mama's future. I was pretty sure she'd hit Grandma right back.

I was pretty sure Grandma knew it, too.

Mama glared at us both through bloodshot eyes. "Stupid superstitious bullshit. Like knots will stop anything."

"A college education doesn't mean you know everything." Grandma's voice was calm, but her chin tilted.

An old argument. Mama left me here when she went to Morgantown on a scholarship. Ever since she came home, she made it plain she didn't like the stuff Grandma had been teaching me while she'd been at college.

My tug on her hand brought Grandma's attention back to me. "Can we watch the stars tonight?"

The lines around her eyes flattened before they crinkled into her familiar grin. She smoothed back the wisps of hair that escaped my ponytail. "Not tonight, Mary Contrary. We need our rest if we're picking strawberries in the morning." She gave a gentle push against my back, sending me in the direction of the staircase.

The wooden legs of Mama's chair screeched as she shoved it back and stood. "Take this piece of hillbilly crap with you." She marched over to the doorframe and yanked the witch's knot off its nail. I caught the yarn flung in my direction.

"Judith—"

A crack and a spray of red interrupted Grandma. Mama spun in the direction of droplets and landed in a heap on the pine planks that made up the kitchen floor.

A growl came from the black silhouette framed by the door. He stepped into the light spilling from the kitchen and kicked aside the remains of the old screen. Something clutched my heart. I couldn't breathe. I'd seen this man before, but only from a distance. Grandpa had been adamant I was not to speak with him. Ever.

"I want my daughter."

Grandma stepped between us. "Get out of here, Jack McGee." Her voice tried to sound strong, but it trembled the same way my arms and legs did.

Most folks were a little afraid of Grandma 'cause she knew stuff. Special stuff, like what knots could do.

The curl of his lip said more than any words. He raised the rifle in his hands.

"Run!"

At Grandma's scream, I twisted and raced for the front stairs. Another crack filled the house. My thumping footsteps up the stairs didn't drown out the wet sounds from the kitchen. The same sounds a watermelon made when the neighbor boys smashed one with baseball bats last summer. The same grunts the boys made while hitting the innocent melon. My stomach heaved.

I tripped over the raised threshold into my room. The throw rug Grandma had woven didn't ease the sharp pain in my knees. Ignoring the ache, I scrambled to my feet and slammed the bedroom door. My toys clattered on the floor when I upended the ancient milk crate holding them. I dragged it over to the doorframe and climbed on top of the hatched plastic. The extra height coupled with my summer growth spurt let me reach the nail in the center, the one that held my lucky clover in a locket. Black yarn caught on steel.

Something crashed into the door and sent me and the milk crate flying across the room. He stood in the open doorway, his chest heaving, the rifle still in his hand. Red smeared his white t-shirt and jeans.

I tried not to think about the red, tried to focus on the knots hanging above his head like Grandma taught me.

"Com'ere, Mary." He tried to soften his voice, but ugliness seeped out of the gravelly tone.

I shook my head and crawled backward in the direction of my bed. I wanted nothing more than to hide under it.

"I'm your father! Get over here now!" Spit sprayed from his mouth. White shone around his pupils. The rank scent of sweat and alcohol filled the room.

Again, I shook my head and huddled against the bed's dust ruffle. Multiple teddy bears smiled their mysterious smile at me as I hid my face in the fabric. Like the black and white yarn hanging above my door, Grandma had filled the ruffle and handmade sheets with protection knots.

"Gahdammit!"

I peered around the ruffle at his hoarse shout. The man lunged at the opening, only to be bounced back. "What the—"

His cursing was interrupted by the pale hands wrapped around his leg. Hands with nothing else attached. One of the hands wore a familiar copper bracelet at its base.

The man's expression shifted from rage, to confusion, to horror. The hands yanked his leg back. His eyes sought mine. "Mary."

My heart didn't budge at his pleading. "Go away!"

He disappeared from the doorway, pulled backward by the disembodied hands. A shriek and a series of thumps echoed up the staircase. After a few moments, I could hear the crickets outside the window over my heartbeat again.

I crawled to the door and peeked out. The hands hovered a foot above the landing, fingers twisting as if tying invisible knots. At the foot of the stairs, the man sprawled, his head twisted in an unnatural angle.

Another moment passed and the knotting hands faded from view. The copper bracelet landed on the pine boards with a clank.

"So then what happened, Aunt Mary?" Madison's eyes were wide as I tucked the covers under her chin. Even though I'd told her this story thousands of times, she always played along.

"I called the police."

She was quiet for a long time before she said, "He

raped your mom too, didn't he? Just like he did my grandma."

I hesitated at her sharp statement of fact. No one talked about the terrible truth in Sweet Water. The habit of silence was as old as the surrounding mountains.

Her tiny hand snaked out from under the sheet and light blanket and rested next to the copper bracelet on my wrist. "It's okay, Aunt Mary. I'm ten. I'm not a baby any more."

I clasped her hand in return. "No, you're not." Neither was I after that night.

A wide yawn split her elfin face. Then she added, "Ya know, even though Grandpa did terrible things, I'm still glad we're family."

My smile at such an innocent sentiment wasn't forced. "G'night, sweetheart." I blew out the candle next to her bed. Tonight of all nights, I wasn't about to take any chances. A quick pat confirmed the tattered black and white knots still hung above my former bedroom door as I headed for the stairs. I'd protect my odd little damaged family.

Gina glanced up from her laptop when I entered the kitchen. "I really wish you wouldn't tell that ancient crap to Madison."

"She needs to know her history." I reached down and yanked the power cord from the outlet next to the china cabinet. "And I said no electricity tonight."

"Hey!" Frantic fingers flew across the keyboard. "My battery's almost dead!"

"Then save your work." I ignored her glare as I moved through the kitchen double-checking that every other appliance was unplugged. The multitude of candles provided more than sufficient light.

"I was e-mailing my husband. You know—the one in Afghanistan?" She slammed the lid shut.

I knew. His term in the service was why my half-sister and niece had been living with me the last several months. I just hadn't planned on him re-enlisting for another stint. Not that I begrudged either of them a place to stay, but my hints to go visit Gina's mother in Wheeling this week had fallen on deaf ears.

She eyed me as I drifted toward the back door to look out. "If this is some weird ritual to observe your family's deaths. . ."

Funny. Gina had never questioned my peculiarities before now. But she was partially right. I'd observed the same scene on this date for years.

Outside, the shadow stood under the ancient pine Grandpa had planted to cover the original outhouse. Just like it had on every June 21st for the last twenty years. Waiting for its opportunity.

The shadow was why Uncle Frank, who had controlled both Mom and Grandma's estates, couldn't keep a renter in the house past the summer solstice, much less sell it. And why I got the house back on my eighteenth birthday. I'd never let the shadow into the house after I moved back in. Bigger knots hung above windows and doors. Tinier knots lay inside outlet and phone covers and adorned the pipes leading into the walls.

Every year on this night since I'd moved back, I huddled in my old bed and listened to his shouts and impotent threats until dawn as he circled the house where he died. And I practiced with macramé twine until blisters carved my skin.

It had taken me all those years to master the last knot Grandma had tried to show me the night of her death.

A whisper of air meant Gina had joined me at the screen door. I paused, questioning if I shouldn't wait until next year. Last thing I wanted was to bring harm to what little family I had left.

"What's going on?"

I turned to face the dark brown eyes so like my own. She stood exactly where Mama had stood twenty years ago. My task couldn't wait. I had the perfect bait. "Gina, do you trust me?"

She blinked at my odd question. "What are you talking about?"

"If you get knocked down, stay down. No matter what happens, stay down. I promise I won't let Madison get hurt." I reached up and yanked the witch's knot from its nail above the backdoor.

The crack of the hunting rifle was as loud as the night my father killed my mother. Gina spun and crashed to the floor.

"Aunt Mary? Mom!"

I whirled to find Madison out of bed, staring at the shadowy figure. "Run!"

Unlike me so long ago, she stood frozen in place, mouth agape.

The second crack threw me into Madison. I tucked and rolled with the girl, praying I didn't hurt her too badly.

Dazed, I looked up. The shadow approached, the ghost rifle raised over its head.

Once again, fear made my stomach heave. I lurched to my feet, half dragging, half carrying a crying Madison toward the stairs. The shadow was so intent on replaying that night it ignored me.

"We have to help Mom!" She began to fight me in earnest, kicking my shins and shredding my skin with her nails.

At the foot of the stairs, I slapped her cheek. She stared at me, and her fingers rose to the darkening mark.

"Get in your room, and don't come out until I tell you." My voice sounded as ugly as my father's had that awful night, but it worked. She pivoted and scrambled up the staircase. I'd apologize later.

If I survived the night.

Diving into the main bedroom to the right of the stairs, I grabbed the half-finished knot work lying on the bed. I exited, only to find the shadow drifting down the hallway. Toward me.

Bone-cold air raised gooseflesh as it passed by me.

I huddled on the floor with the three balls of twine and my sharpest shears. Finding the red yarn more by touch than sight, my fingers tied the last three knots and sliced the cotton string. "May you pay for the harm you caused in life, Jack McGee." It was the first time I ever spoke my father's name aloud.

At the first landing, the shadow tried to enter my old bedroom. Forced back by the charm over the door, it beat against the invisible wall with its black fists. From inside, Madison screamed for me, her mother, anyone.

Black twine encased the red, tied and cut. "May you pay for the harm you caused in death, Jack McGee."

The copper bracelet glinted, but there was nothing in the dark hallway to reflect off it. I ignored the odd light the same way I had to ignore Madison's cries for help.

The black twine went inside the white. Two knots almost finished the job. "Jack McGee, I bind you from bothering the living or the dead ever again." It would be the last time I ever said his name.

An anguished scream echoed through the stairwell, the shadow's deep bass, not Madison's high-pitched wail. It crumpled under my words and thoughts, its form running down the stairs like creek water skipping over stones. Black fog flowed into the little makeshift bag. Without a thought, I twisted the final knot in place.

My little peace was short-lived. Gina flicked the

hallway light on and stared at me. "What the hell just happened?"

I had no idea how to answer. I should already be in a straight jacket according to half of our tiny town.

She shuffled down the hall. With a muffled grunt, she slid down the wall until she sat next to me. "So that was dear old dad, huh?" Sarcasm laced her tone as she rubbed the spot on her chest where the ghost bullet had struck her. I should have known she'd figure things out.

"Mom?"

At the tentative whisper from above us, Gina called, "It's okay, baby. It's over."

Not even the rustle of bare feet on the pine boards.

A smile tugged at the corners of my lips. Good girl. She obeyed me. "C'mon down, Madison."

Little white feet flew down the steps, and Madison launched herself into Gina's arms.

Gina eyed the knotted bag in my hand over her daughter's dark locks. "What do we do with that?"

I fingered twine that was far heavier than it should be. "We take it to the cemetery."

Gina raised a quizzical eyebrow. "Bury it with the rest of him?"

My smile became earnest. "No. Grandma's grave. She'll make sure it's never found." The copper bracelet on my wrist winked in agreement.

Love Train

The dorky-looking guy with black plastic hipster eyeglasses and shaggy brown hair sitting two rows in front of me on the subway car had to have used an entire bottle of a popular body spray. The odor was so bad I could taste the chemicals. My eyes watered, and my nose was about to drip as my allergies kicked into high gear. I reached into my purse for tissue only to discover the travel-sized pack I carried with me was gone.

Dammit, Dean! My husband took mine rather than add tissues to the grocery list hanging on the refrigerator.

The subway train brakes half-hummed, half-whistled as we slowed. The PA crackled to life. "Next stop, Twinbrook Station."

I couldn't last all the way to the Smithsonian stop on the Metro. At least, not in this car. A desperate search of my jacket pockets produced a napkin from my favorite Chinatown restaurant. I blew my nose, loud enough the twenty or so other passengers all stared at me, including Body Spray Guy. I'd get off at Twinbrook and move to another car.

Or better yet, wait for the next train.

For all of my family's magical talents, there should be a spell to counteract allergies. My mother claimed my issues were because of all the modern living conveniences. No one let their children play in the dirt and become attuned to nature.

I played in the dirt plenty as a child, and I was definitely attuned to nature. That's how I kept cockroaches out of our townhouse in Montgomery Village. It sure didn't stop me from developing hay fever in college.

If I waited for the next train though, I'd be late for my appointment with Doctor Goss. But he'd be even more peeved if I sneezed all over his research, even if I was the top forensic archeologist on this side of the country.

However, when the subway train stopped at Twinbrook, the platform was packed. Twinbrook was never packed this late in the morning. If I got out of the car, I'd never get back on.

The doors slid open, and people flooded into the car. More of a crowd gathered on the platform. An older lady in an obvious mourning dress plunked down on the seat beside me, the scent of cigarettes wafting from her clothes and hair.

"What's going on?" I gestured at the disappointed faces outside the window as the PA warned to keep clear of the doors.

"Big accident on Rockville Pike," she murmured. "All lanes are closed. With the backup, I couldn't get to the Beltway, and I am not missing my auntie's funeral."

The doors hissed shut, and the subway surged forward. There went my plan to change trains. I couldn't even change cars with the people packed inside. I would have thought the sheer amount of bodies would mitigate Body Spray Guy's odor.

My seatmate wrinkled her nose. "Please tell me that's not you, honey."

I was impressed she could smell him through her own smoke and nicotine odors. "Two seats in front of us," I whispered before I tried to discretely sniff. Between the two of them, I'd never make it to the Smithsonian without snot dripping down my face.

The lady glanced at the wadded napkin in my fist before she reached into her purse. She handed me a travel size pack of tissues.

"Thank you," I murmured as I pulled a tissue out and handed the pack back to her.

However, she didn't respond while she absently stuck the tissues into her purse. Her gaze was glued on the hipster doofus and the man sitting beside him. Their heads were bent together, and they shot furtive glances around them.

I'd been married to a narcotics detective long enough to know when a questionable deal was going down.

"Bokor," my seatmate whispered.

A chill ran through me. A Vodoun sorcerer for hire.

They'd do a spell for any purpose and for any reason if you met their price.

I eyed my seatmate and mouthed, "Mambo?"

She shook her head, not taking her eyes off the two men. "No, Auntie was though." If her aunt was a Vodoun priestess, my seatmate was probably an adherent, too. Contrary to what most people thought, the Vodou religion was practiced throughout the country. One of the things I loved about D.C. was the little bit of everything that constructed its culture.

Well, the normal people anyway. No one who actually lives in the D.C. metropolitan area counts the politicians.

"Latoya." My seatmate looked at me. I could tell the instant she noticed the tiny pentacles in my ears. To her credit, she didn't flinch and pull away.

I smiled at her. Shaking hands had gone out of style with the pandemic a decade ago. "Reece."

She grinned. "Like the peanut butter cups?"

Yeah, that was the joke everyone made. I merely grinned back. "My husband's the chocolate."

Latoya cracked up. A few of people standing in the aisle gave her funny looks, but at least, she wasn't offended by my joke. People still got stupid about mixed marriages. If they only knew I was mixed in a different way.

She lowered her voice with her next question. "Can you tell what he's selling to the other guy?"

Part of me hoped it was drugs. All I had to do was

text the transit police for a human crime. If the two men were exchanging some spell, potion, or talisman though, I might accidentally give myself away. Did I really want a bokor's attention? They had a reputation for not playing nice. But if he was selling something innocent like a good luck charm, neither man would be acting squirrelly.

I closed my eyes and concentrated. My second sight kicked in and I wanted to groan. It was definitely magic. A love potion. I hated those things. They were the magical equivalent of a roofie. They disrupted the free will of the person who it was cast upon.

My eyes opened to find the bokor and the hipster doofus staring at me. I smiled and waved at them. Beside me, Latoya muttered, "Oh, shit, the kid's gonna bolt."

The train braked as we glided toward the White Flint Station. The platform was just as packed here as Twinbrook had been.

Latoya was right. The hipster doofus shoved the potion bottle back at the bokor, jumped to his feet, and vaulted onto the laps of the elderly couple in the seat in front of him. She shrieked. He tried to grab the doofus, who wiggled out of the older man's grasp. People numbly stared at the chaos, only protesting when the hipster doofus pushed past them and darted through the opening car doors.

The hipster doofus wasn't the big problem though. The scowling bokor had risen and was making his way back to us. A couple of passengers grabbed his vacated seat while other people tried to enter the car from the crush on the platform.

"What the hell?" he roared over the PA announcement to clear the doors.

Latoya surged out of her seat. "Maybe you shouldn't be conducting business on the subway." She jabbed a finger in his chest as the subway train started moving south again. "I asked her what you was doing because it sure looked like a drug deal from back here."

Despite her being easily his weight, he glared at me and tried to push past her. "You owe me the money I just lost."

I narrowed my eyes and scowled right back at him as the doors slid shut. If he wanted a scene, I'd definitely oblige. It wasn't like he was going anywhere.

"First of all, you blew your own deal by looking at me and acting guilty. Your buyer was already on edge from breathing in the fumes of an entire bottle of body spray." That set a few people around us snickering. "Second of all, you were selling him a roofie."

The folks surrounding us, even the elderly couple trying desperately to ignore the altercation, all turned to look at him.

Realizing we had an audience, he growled under his breath, "A love potion is not the same thing."

The elderly woman turned to her husband. "Is 'love potion' the new slang for the date-rape drug?" Her question prompted another round of snickering from the other passengers. The husband's ears flushed bright pink.

"Pay me my lost fee," the bokor repeated.

"Or what?" Latoya poked him in the chest again.

The train's brakes hummed as we approached the Grosvenor platform. When the bokor grinned, a sick feeling gathered in my gut. He pulled the bottle from his jacket pocket and thumbed off the lid.

"The bottle!" I jumped to my feet and tried to grab it from his hand.

I was too late. Liquid splashed on me, Latoya and a bunch of other passengers. The bokor threw the bottle at my head. I ducked, and it shattered against the wall behind me. The bokor whirled around and shoved his way past the standing passengers in the direction of the opening doors.

He wasn't getting away that easily. I hexed the doors for our car, and they slammed shut. One of the men standing in the aisle pressed the bokor against the door and twisted his arm into some kind of locking hold. The bokor shouted a stream of invectives, but from his grimace, he couldn't break free without something getting pulled from its sockets.

The subway train slid into motion again. There were a lot of angry passengers on the platform, but they didn't know how lucky they were.

"What was that liquid?" one of the tourists asked.

His companion sniffed her sleeve. "At least, it's not pee."

Latoya and I exchanged worried looks. I could detect the potion's intent, but I didn't know if it was something that needed to be consumed or if it worked another way.

The older woman plowed through the other riders to reach the bokor. I followed in her wake.

"You ladies okay?" The guy holding the bokor had some serious muscles showing through his own hoodie. "Did he threaten you?"

"Yes." Latoya pulled a phone from her purse and started tapping 9-1-1. But just as her thumb moved to send the call, I felt a push of magic. The device sizzled and shot out sparks. Latoya cried out and dropped the phone.

The bokor grinned through the pain of his wrenched shoulder and elbow. "You've got other things to worry about besides me."

I looked over my shoulder. The elderly couple were already making out like they were teenagers again. Everyone else splashed by the potion had dazed looks. I was shaking, but it wasn't from the potion's effects on me. Part of me wanted to test the reality of transfiguration, that is, turn the bastard into a newt.

I turned back to the bokor. "How do we neutralize the potion?"

"Potion?" The guy holding the bokor frowned.

"You're the witch." The bokor's grin mocked my demand. "Can't you do it?"

I considered my options. Without knowing what

was in the potion, any counteragent could make the effects worse. Not that I had any ingredients with me on the subway to begin with. If I used raw power, he might be able to twist it since it was his own magic causing the problem.

"Would this help?" Latoya pulled a small item from her suit pocket. "My auntie made it for me." She dropped the tiny white cotton bag in my hand. Several hard objects were tied inside.

A juju bag. The protective magic was why she wasn't affected by the bokor's potion.

"No!" The bokor struggled against the guy holding him.

I grinned. "That'll do just fine."

The bokor voice changed to a purr. "You love me. You all love me. You'll do anything to protect me—"

"Shut him up!" But my warning came too late. The other passengers the potion had touched, except for the elderly couple who were now struggling to remove their jackets, turned to me in unison.

The guy holding the bokor muttered an obscenity.

"What's going on?" a woman standing toward the front of the car asked with alarm.

"That asshole drugged the passengers in the back of the car." Latoya pointed at the bokor. "They don't know what they're doing. Move to the front of the car so you're not affected. Someone call 9-1-1." She herded folks forward despite the tight space to give me some room to work. Several people were calling for emergency services. Others texted or e-mailed for help. The bokor couldn't hex all of their phones before a message got through.

I got on the other side of the bokor and his captor, where the sorcerer couldn't see what was in the tiny bag. I dumped the contents into my damp palm. A small spool from a sewing machine with white thread wound on it. An antique ebony domino with four and three dots. A blue agate marble. A sprig of dried white sage. Good. I could use these. I started tying a pattern with the thread.

"Save me, my loves! The witch is trying to kill me!" the bokor shouted.

Those passengers affected by the potion surged forward. The guy holding the bokor glanced at me before he released the bokor and plowed into the affected passengers to keep them from attacking me. They all went down in a mass of flailing limbs. The weird thing was the silence from the people affected by the potion. It was a good thing the hipster doofus hadn't gotten away with the vial. Goddess only knew what would have happened to the person he planned to use it on.

Unfortunately, everyone falling on the floor and seats gave me a good view of the elderly couple. If I didn't break this spell soon, they'd be arrested for indecent exposure if they didn't accidentally kill themselves with their acrobatics.

Muttering the words of the binding spell, I tied the last knot in the thread. The bokor charged toward me.

I skipped back a step. The bokor tripped over his own untied shoelace and banged his head against the center pole with a resounding *BONG* just when the train slowed as it approached the Medical Center station. He collapsed to the floor, unconscious. This time though, there were police and medical personnel standing on the platform as we whizzed by.

We couldn't let the affected passengers go. Goddess only knew what else that potion would do to them. Luckily, the train's braking system was linked between all the cars.

Once again, I concentrated and hexed both the braking system and the automatic safety shutdown. The train pick up speed and whipped through the station to the amazement of the first responders standing on the platform. The hexes would only last until the Bethesda station, but hopefully it would give me the few minutes I needed.

Unfortunately, the guy who'd tried to help me was having trouble keeping the passengers under the potion's influence contained to the back of the car by himself. Latoya pushed past me and pulled something metallic from her purse. In a second, she'd cuffed the bokor and took a step towards the guy awkwardly struggling with those affected by the love potion.

"Wait!"

At my shout, she paused.

"I need your lighter or matches."

She tossed me her purse. "In there." She waded into the battle at the back of the car.

I dropped to the floor by the bokor's head and assumed a cross-legged position. Thank goodness D.C. Metro kept their cars cleaner than some other subway systems I'd ridden on. I laid the domino on the floor and set the marble on top. The little disposable butane lighter was in the outside pocket of Latoya's purse along with half a pack of cigarettes. The marble rolled with the slight motion of the subway train.

Latoya threw herself against the magic-affected crowd. They were on the verge of overwhelming my two saviors. Well, all of the folks except the elderly couple who only had eyes for each other.

Lighting the white sage, I whispered the cleansing spell. Smoke swirled into the air and spread through the car. Ashes dropped onto the marble. Whispers came from the people behind me. My grandmother, mom, and aunts would kick my ass for casting in public, but my conscience couldn't let anything happen to the innocent people affected by the bokor's potion.

With my attention on the cleansing spell, my hex on the brake lines died. The conductor regained control of the train. We slowed but continued moving.

The folks bespelled by the potion stopped trying to get by Latoya and the guy who helped us. They all seemed confused, except the elderly couple. They both turned beet red, and the husband pulled his coat over his wife while she attempted to straighten her clothes.

As we pulled into the Bethesda station, the platform was filled with first responders. I blew the ashes off the marble and domino before I returned them and what was left of the white thread to Latoya's juju bag. I started sneezing like crazy from the sage smoke as the train drew to a gentle stop.

A couple of hours later, the bokor had been hauled off to the closest police substation. Luckily, the officer in charge had been one of Dean's classmates at the academy. Well, that, and the fact the other passengers corroborated mine and Latoya's stories about the bokor and his buyer's odd behavior.

I'd called Doctor Goss to reschedule our appointment. He'd heard about the subway incident so he wasn't too peeved about my absence.

Unfortunately, sitting outside the Bethesda station on a bench, waiting for my rideshare, with cherry blossoms, forsythia, and every other spring pollen in the air wasn't helping my allergies. After a sneezing fit, I didn't have anything left so I resorted to wiping my nose on my sleeve.

"Now that's just uncivilized."

I looked up to find Latoya standing in front of me and holding out her travel-sized tissue pack.

"Danks," I muttered.

"Keep the whole pack, honey." She chuckled as she

dropped in the seat beside me. "I think you're going to need it."

After I blew my nose, I murmured, "I'm sorry you missed your aunt's funeral."

"So am I." Latoya sighed. "But I had my chance to say goodbye before she passed."

I pulled my phone out of my pocket. "Could I please have your address and phone number? I'll replace the sage for your juju bag."

She eyed me a moment before she pulled out a business card. "Actually, I was going to ask you if you were interested in some part-time work."

"Part-time work?" I took the card and read it. "Colton Retrieval Specialists." I looked up at her. "You're a bounty hunter?"

"Actually, it is my auntie and cousins' business." Latoya shrugged. "I handle the bookkeeping and the phones, but you could help the boys with finding their bounties. How are you with lost people or lost object spells?"

"Are you—are you offering me a job?"

"What do you do now?" she asked.

"I'm a consulting forensic archeologist." I grinned.

She whistled. "Well, we can't match your salary, but you could pick up some cash with a side hustle."

Something said there was more to this than helping with bounty hunting. "You're not only retrieving non-magical people, are you?"

"No." Latoya smiled. "But you handled yourself

pretty good with that bokor. Like I said, the boys could use someone like you. Besides, it wouldn't hurt us to have a friendly cop on the side. I overheard your chocolate was a boy in blue."

I laughed. "You are incorrigible."

"Is that a yes or a no?" she asked.

"More like let me talk it over with my husband." I cocked my head. "And I think you need to talk it over with your cousins."

"Already texted them, Peanut Butter." Latoya held up her phone. "How about you and your husband join us for dinner tomorrow night? You can bring over that white sage you owe me."

I wasn't the action junkie she thought I was, but it wouldn't hurt to talk to her cousins. My career might just take an exciting and unexpected turn. One I might enjoy as much if not more than my work at the Smithsonian.

I smiled. "It's a date."

Unexpected

The dragon arrived the same drizzly late spring day the basket with the human baby appeared on my doorstep.

I had been brewing a remedy for the illness that had most of our village in its feverish grip. The slow drip of the eaves had paused for the barest of instances, but I couldn't say what drew my attention. I set down my spoon. I'd opened the front shutters to clear the hot steam and potentially soporific fumes. Yet, I hadn't noticed anyone approach my home.

Maybe I should have opened the door when I started cooking as well.

When I checked outside, the bamboo basket sat on my stoop. It was covered in a fine gray wool. The rain-washed stone walkway Shang had laid for me two years ago showed no evidence of passage. Not even a speck of mud from the road.

I poked my head around the corner of the wood and brick front that kept the elements from my cave. The carved stairway to the top of the cliff was empty as well.

Interesting. I knelt and pulled the blanket aside. The infant was only a day or three old at most. It smacked its lips together and squirmed a bit.

The cabbages planted in my garden rustled. I froze and waited. It didn't sound like the rabbits, and there was too much daylight, even with the overcast sky, to be one of the night scavengers.

"Why don't you come out of there?" I said. "The mud cannot be that comfortable."

A black head with a white mane and markings poked out from under a leaf. The dragon was tiny, its skull barely the size of my fist. A baby itself.

I cocked my head and pointed at the basket. "Did you bring it?"

Its ebony eyelids slid down over its golden eyes and rose.

"Talkative one, aren't you?"

Another slow blink.

I tried a different tactic. "Are you hungry?"

The dragon sneezed, and its black whiskers curled and relaxed. It sinuously unwound itself from my cabbages and approached me on its four tiny legs.

"I am Fen," I said and held out my hand.

In an adult dragon, the gift of my name would have been sufficient decorum, but this wasn't a usual situation. Its whiskers tickled my skin as it tested my truthfulness. I waited until the dragon was satisfied. It may not be able to incinerate me yet, but its bite would still be painful. It finished its examination with a lick of its rough tongue on my palm and trill of approval. I returned the compliment by scratching its mane and the white spiked ridge along its spine.

The poor thing must have been terribly desperate to come to a human for help. I eyed the human baby. The dragon hooked its front claws on the edge of the basket and peered inside, then looked up at me.

A recent edict by the new emperor worried me more than I cared to admit. Only the imperial family were allowed in the presence of dragons. For all his power, he might as well tell the wind not to blow. Dragons went where they wished and did exactly what they wanted.

That didn't mean the emperor wouldn't take out his displeasure on any innocent human who was approached by a dragon.

I grasped the handles of the basket and rose. "First thing to do is check the baby for fertilizer."

The dragon followed me inside and headed straight for the fire. It curled up on the hearthstones with an almost human sigh of contentment.

I found a clean cloth that could serve as a diaper and replaced the wet one the infant wore. While I couldn't tell the gender of the dragon, the baby was male and slightly malnourished. Had the dragon taken him the moment he was born? If so, why?

I diced three dried fish, placed them on my best plate, and served the dragon. It daintily picked up the first hunk and bowed to me before it devoured all the fish with a speed I'd only seen in Shang's sons as they entered manhood.

After pulling the cauldron with the fever remedy from the fire, I retrieved the urn of milk from the spring deeper in the cave that formed part of my home. Using another clean cloth, I coaxed the baby into sucking milk. What he really needed was a wet nurse, but that was impossible until the sickness in the village had been dealt with.

The dragon flopped on its back over the plate, its distended belly reaching for the roof beams extending from the cliff face. By the time the infant in my arms burped, the dragon's snores filled the air.

My guests woke from their naps shortly after I'd transferred the cooled potion to two skins. I fed them once again.

I frowned as the dragon waited patiently by the front door. "I don't suppose I can convince you to stay here while I go to the village."

Again, the slow blink of its golden eyes.

I didn't like my choices. The human infant couldn't stay here. While I'd warded my dwelling against supernatural elements, my kitchen magics wouldn't keep out conventional intruders or predators. If I tried to lock the dragon inside, it would no doubt destroy my meager belongings in its efforts to escape. Not to mention the insult I'd cause to an ancient and venerable race.

And while our tiny village was at the farthest edge of the empire, I worried of what may happen if word of the dragon spread beyond our province.

"If you insist on accompanying me, will you please stay out of sight?"

Its whiskers fluttered.

"And you will need to stay with the human infant at a friend's home while I deliver medicine to the rest of the village."

It wasn't as enthusiastic about that condition, but it curled and released its whiskers in acquiescence. I half-expected the dragon to balk at me carrying him in my double chest sling.

Once both babies were snug and settled, I hefted the bamboo pole over my shoulders, the full skins swaying slightly at the ends, and marched through the drizzle toward the village.

The silence unnerved me when we reached the first buildings. The tanner's and the butcher's businesses normally hummed with activity even on such a dreary day. No pigs played in the mud. No chickens clucked under the awnings. Not even the oxen lowed in their barns.

The baby started to fuss, and the dragon nuzzled the tiny human. Its actions calmed the infant, but its whiskers curled tight against its muzzle. So I wasn't the only one concerned over the unnatural quiet.

Was the illness far worse than I believed when I'd departed the village late last night? I left the main road for the path leading to the quarry. Like my own cave, Shang's cottage was far away enough not to be part of the village out of necessity.

Even on a rainy day such as this, hammers should have rung from his workshop. Had the twins come down with the illness, too? I approached the living quarters and caught the sounds of retching. Rather than politely announcing myself, I burst into the cottage.

Shang held Bao, his eldest Xian's fiancée, with one hand over a bucket as her stomach relieved itself. His other hand held her braid out of the way. His own black and silver hair was loose and unkempt, and his arms trembled with effort.

I set the skins and pole on the wooden floor. "When did she become sick?"

"Only a little while ago," Shang answered for the girl. Her vomiting had turned to dry heaves. "Bao stayed the night caring for us."

I'd assumed that much from the haphazard pallet she was propped on. I divested myself of the slings and laid the bundles on the low table the family used for meals. The dragon poked his head out and stretched.

"What—" Bao rasped out as Shang settled her back on the blankets.

He turned and caught sight of my latest responsibility, and his face lit up with surprise and delight. "Greetings, honored one." He tried to bow. It was a good thing he was already sitting because he fell over.

I helped him upright so he could scoot back and lean against the wall. His skin burned through his clothes. I checked Bao. Her fever was just as bad.

"Do all four boys have the illness now?" I asked as I strode across the room to the shelves where Shang kept his dishes.

"Yes."

That explained the quiet. I was probably the only person in the entire village still standing. But in all my predecessor's teachings, I'd never heard of a disease that moved this fast through a population.

Only a couple of chipped cups were remotely clean and serviceable. I retrieve one of the skins and proceeded to dilute my potion with a bottle of rice wine I found.

"I was saving that for a special occasion," Shang teased.

"You didn't specify what type of occasion to the gods," I said. "I think this qualifies." I handed a cup to him and helped Bao raise her head to drink.

She collapsed back on the pallet when I heard the baby gurgle.

"Fen?" Both Shang and the dragon were looking

inside the second bundle of cloth. Shang looked up at me with a puzzle expression. "Is there something you neglected to tell me?"

"He's not yours." I mock frowned. "At least, he's not yours by me."

Shang lifted the baby and cradled the child in his arms.

"You shouldn't have brought the baby here, Mistress Fen." Bao's fever-bright eyes bore into me. "This illness—"

"I didn't have much of a choice," I said more sharply than I intended. "The baby and the dragon appeared on my doorstep this morning with no explanation."

"Someone may have been trying to get him away from the village," Shang said quietly.

"It's too late. From the lack of activity I saw on my way here, everyone's sick now." I took the two cups and mixed more medicine to take to the boys. "Can you please watch him while I make my rounds? I'll find out who he belongs to and return him."

"I will if you would be kind enough to feed our animals." A spark of Shang's normal humor appeared in his weak smile.

"Always have to push the bargain, don't you?" I smiled back.

What little humor I'd dredged disappeared after I'd given his sons their medicine and approached the small barn Shang kept for his team of oxen, a few pigs and a flock of chickens. The stench that assaulted my nose had nothing to do with the animals' waste.

I eased the wide wooden door open. Flies were the only activity inside. They buzzed around the still, silent forms. The dead livestock provided the mute witnesses for the truth I'd been denying for the last day. Our home had been cursed.

After my discovery, I went from house to house as fast as my feet could carry me. In many cases, the youngest, the oldest, and the most infirm were as dead as so many of the animals. And I was right.

I was the only person in the village who hadn't taken ill. Nor could the few with some mobility deal with the dead. After an argument with Chief Po, which was cut short by his vomiting, I raised the plague flags on the road at each end of the village to prevent more victims. No sense alarming anyone else with my suspicions.

Near sunset, I trudged through the rain back to Shang's property with my empty skins, believing I would never be dry again. I barely had enough medicine for those still alive and needed to brew more. Caring for the ill would make it impossible for me to track down who had cast the curse and stop it. My other option was to let more of my fellows die in order to save the rest.

When I entered his cottage, Shang, his sons and Bao

sat around their low table. Their skin countenance was pale and wan, but they appeared in far better spirits than when I had left hours ago. The place no longer smelled of sickness. Instead, the odor of vegetable broth teased a rumble of hunger from my stomach.

"Come sit with us, Fen." Shang patted the cushion to his right. A place of honor in any household.

Heat flooded my cheeks as I set down my gear. Our relationship was one of convenience. I had no intention of ever becoming his wife, and I appreciated the freedom being the village's wise woman afforded me. Shang, on the other hand, had no wish to disgrace his wife's memory in front of their children. Yet, here he was, offering me a seat at his family's table.

"Please, join us, Mistress Fen," his youngest Daquan piped up.

I bowed. "Thank you for your hospitality."

As I knelt next to Shang, a mewl came from the basket beside Bao. "Hungry, again?"

"Here," Xian said, holding out his hands for the baby. "I'll feed him while you dish some stew for Mistress Fen."

I squelched the urge to jump to my feet. To do so would have been incredibly rude on my part. Instead, I tried to focus on the problems before me. "Where is the dragon?"

Daquan giggled. "He's asleep in my lap. I took him to the stream after my fever broke. He was so funny catching the fish."

As if the dragon knew they were discussing him, a black head with a white mane peered over the table surface. Sleepy golden eyes blinked before he sank back into Daquan's lap.

"How do you know he's male?" I asked.

Daquan shrugged. "I just do." He stroked the dragon's white mane. "Have you named him yet, Mistress Fen?"

I chuckled as Bao handed me a bowl. Bits of last summer's carrots and fresh spring cabbage floated in the broth. My stomach growled again.

"We do not name dragons. They will gift us their names if they believe we are worthy." The first mouthful of soup was so good I wanted to drain the bowl in one long swallow.

Daquan cocked his head and regarded the dragon in his lap. "I think I will call you Jin for your gold eyes."

I would have sworn I heard the dragon purr.

The family discussed the necessity of replacing the oxen while the baby and I ate our respective dinners. But such things were not to be unless I discovered the source of the curse.

"You've honored me with your hospitality," I said. "But I need to return home in order to brew another batch for tomorrow. Not everyone in the village are as strong as Shang the stone cutter and his sons." I rose from the table.

The dragon poured himself from Daquan's lap and raced for the door. He whirled to face me and hissed.

I propped my fists on my hips. "What has gotten into you?"

He hissed again in response.

I took a step toward the door.

The dragon growled and thin wisps of smoke drifted from his nostrils.

Shang rose and gently grasped my arm. "I think the three of you are spending the night here after all. I'll go with you in the morning to your cave to retrieve whatever you need."

"You're still recovering," I protested.

"And you'll wear yourself out at this pace,"

"But—" My gaze swiveled between Shang and the dragon before exhaustion made me sag in defeat. "Very well."

Shang started barking orders. "Xian and Bao, you take my bed tonight. You two are on baby duty."

Bao reddened at his scandalous suggestion, and Xian stammered.

Shang held up his hand. "You two are going to be wed in three weeks anyway. And tonight, you'll discover how much your lives will change when you have your own child." He turned to the twins. "Yuanjun, Zhen, bring Xian's pallet out here for Mistress Fen."

Despite the unintentional slow pace caused by everyone's weakness, accommodations were quickly arranged. The younger members of the clan were soon in bed. Shang banked the fire against the night's chill before he claimed the makeshift pallet Bao had used the night before.

"This is the first time we've spent the night together," he said as he stretched out.

I chuckled. "Too bad you're still recovering, and I'm too tired."

"The joys of getting older." He rolled to face me and propped his head on his arm. "How bad?" His dark eyes reflected glowing coals and my worry.

I shook my head and told him of what I'd seen and heard. Of what I suspected.

"That doesn't make sense. Why would anyone curse our village? We have nothing anyone but ourselves would want."

"We have my visitors." I twisted my body to check the dragon. He still sat primly in front of the door, as still as his stone counterparts Shang's great-great-grandfather had carved that guarded the village shrine. Only the occasional blink of his golden eyes showed any life.

"And no one claimed the infant?"

I turned back to Shang, but I couldn't meet his gaze. The idea I'd put him and his family in danger by bringing the baby and the dragon here gnawed at me. "I wasn't forthright in my questioning, but every woman who had a child within the last month had her child with her."

Even the two who had lost theirs to this curse, but I couldn't say the words aloud. I stared at the light dancing on the wall opposite of the fire hearth. "He definitely comes from someplace else, but the gods only know where, or why he was brought here."

"I think you already know the answer to the last one, my love. The dragon needs your help to guard the child."

The dragon didn't hiss or growl when Shang and I left the cottage shortly after dawn. Before Shang shut the door, I saw the little black and white form crawl under the blanket I had straightened moments before.

Fog had rolled in after yesterday's warm rain. Shang breathed deeply. From his grimace, he got a whiff of his bad fortune. "I don't suppose there's any use I can make of the meat."

"I wouldn't recommend salvaging any parts since I'm not sure what exactly we dealing with. It would be best if we burned the carcasses."

"I suggest you gather everything you might need for the next few days," Shang added.

"Being a little overprotective, aren't you?" I glared at him.

"No. I'm heeding the dragon's warning." He headed for the narrow track that cut around the quarry to a shared pasture, instead of the wider path to the village.

"Why are we going this way?" True this was a shorter route, but the thorn thicket after the plum orchard needed constant trimming to make it passable for more than one person at a time.

"It's prudence, not overprotectiveness, which drives me. The dragon didn't want you going home last night."

I eyed him as we trod in the tracks where his oxen had worn away the grass. "Your theory was he needed me to help him protect the baby."

Shang shrugged. "How can you help him if you're at risk?"

I shook my head. "You're as stubborn as your stones." But I followed him anyway.

It turned out Shang's caution was warranted. We heard the horses before we reached the steps cut into the cliff face that housed my cave.

He held his finger to his lips and dropped to his stomach, gesturing for me to do the same. Swallowing my displeasure at crawling through the dew and rain-soaked scrub, I followed him until we could peer over the edge.

I clapped a hand over my mouth to stifle a gasp. Below us were a dozen soldiers. A pennant in imperial red hung limply in the morning's still air. Another man wore the cloak and cylindrical hat of the bureaucracy. The last figure was the one that truly concerned me. He wore the gold robes of a court sorcerer.

A good deal of my herb and seed stock was scattered,

their respective jars smashed against the stones of the walkway Shang had laid. Uprooted plants from my garden showed their roots to the sun. The soldiers poked through the damage or fed the tender greens to their steeds.

The bureaucrat and the sorcerer's heads bent over something. When the sorcerer tossed the first page and it fluttered to the ground, I realized he held the notes I'd left on my worktable yesterday.

"I don't understand it!" The bureaucrat flung away the scroll he examined.

A scroll that had been handed down through the years by those of us in the village with the gift. Anger heated my blood.

"How could a mere village witch hide them from you!"

The sorcerer's head rose, and the soldiers backed away from the bureaucrat. "She couldn't."

"And if your curse worked, she should be lying here dead!"

The sorcerer flicked a long fingernail against the scroll he held. "This is a recipe for a fever reducer. She probably collapsed in the village, dying with the rest of her people."

"Then where is the prince and that gods-be-damned dragon!"

"We go to the village and search house by house."

"That will take time," one of soldiers said. From the more ornate embroidery on his cloak, he must be their captain. "The dragon's probably moved on to the next village by now."

Shang tugged on my arm, and we carefully crawled away from the cliff. Once we were out of earshot, we ran for the thorn thicket. We had to slow when we reached it, but from his labored breathing, it was a necessity. After what we'd witnessed, I'd forgotten how sick he had been for the last two days.

We reached the plum orchard before I felt safe enough to speak. "How am I going to brew more medicine, much less get it to the village?"

"You can't. A simple medicine won't stop the curse," Shang said between huffing breaths.

"I'll take the dragon and the baby, and head south for the capital." I took a step. "If the curse follows us, everyone still alive should recover."

Shang's hand clamped around my wrist. "No. Jin spirited the prince out of the palace for a reason."

"One he either can't or won't reveal," I argued. "But if they stay at your cottage, your sons' lives—" I couldn't say the rest. The consequences were too terrible to contemplate.

He squeezed my wrist until the bones ached, which was unlike him. "Fen, you are the smartest, most practical person I know. Is there a way to break this curse? Because it sounds like that sorcerer is using it to track the pair. If so, he'll be able to follow you until you succumb and die."

"Shang," I said quietly. "You're hurting me."

He released my arm, but said nothing. Dark eyes bore into me.

I rubbed my wrist. "That's the reason I wanted to go back last night. To retrieve my scrolls."

"And if you'd been there when those soldiers arrived—"

I was sure my smile looked as weak as it felt. "You're saying the dragon saved my life?"

"Think about it, Fen." He stared in the direction of the quarry before he turned back to me. "Why would a dragon take an imperial prince?"

"They've always sworn to protect . . ." Shang's point sank past my panic. Oh gods! What had those men planned to do to the baby? "I'm no match for a fully-trained sorcerer!"

He crossed his arms. "I'll tell you the same thing I tell Daquan when he says a stone is too large to be shaped. You—"

"Start with one chip at a time," I finished. A deep, cleansing breath didn't banish all my fear, but it allowed a glimmer of hope I might come up with a solution.

By the time we reached Shang's cottage, a token plan bloomed in my mind. If I couldn't break the curse, I needed to turn it back on the caster. With the determination of the sorcerer and the bureaucrat we witnessed, they would surely appear on Shang's doorstep sooner rather than later.

I put the three oldest boys to work while their father rested. They dealt with the disposal of the animal carcasses other than the parts I'd requested. Bao assisted me in preparing what for us was a feast. The girl even allowed me to use some of the seeds that were to be part of her bridal gift. Daquan assisted by caring for the baby.

The dragon was another matter entirely.

While Bao chopped the new greens we had collected, I picked him up from where he warmed himself on the window sill. He crawled up my arm and draped himself over my shoulder as I walked outside.

I took a deep breath. "Honorable One, the men who are after you and the prince are in the village. We have a plan, but I must ask you some questions. I understand your duty to the prince. I hope I have earned your trust enough that you will answer my questions truthfully. All of our lives depend on it."

He nodded.

"Is the curse afflicting the village attached to you?"

He nodded again.

"Is it attached to the baby?"

He shook his head.

"Is the curse activated when you use your magic?"

Another nod.

"Why wasn't Shang and his family affected more severely by the curse?"

The dragon butted my cheek with his head.

"Because of me?"

Another nod.

I stared at the dark column of smoke that rose from the quarry and dissected the brilliant blue sky as I tried to formulate my concerns. We'd seen similar fires from the south all day. My abilities were meager compared to a formally trained sorcerer. He obviously didn't care about the damage his curse had wrought on so many innocents.

"Because of my magic?" I finally said.

The dragon reached up and patted my temple with the pad of his clawed hand. Then, he crawled across my chest and patted my breastbone. Gold eyes stared into mine.

My heart pounded beneath his five clawed fingers. "My magic mitigated the effects of the curse because I care about them?"

His whiskers waved enthusiastically. He crawled up to my left shoulder and pointed at the door to the cottage.

No, not the door itself. The characters I'd carved into the lintel. Protection. Peace. Prosperity.

Would my affection for Shang and his family be enough to save them? Or had I doomed us all?

Jin rubbed his head against my cheek.

"I hope you're right," I whispered.

The steady beat of hooves thrummed through the stone under me. I rose from my kneeling position at the family's shrine. The sun was a handspan above the horizon. I silently sent a prayer to the gods the sorcerer hadn't harmed the rest of our friends who had survived the initial effects of the curse.

Shang approached the men and bowed. "How may a humble stone cutter serve the emperor?"

The captain of the guard kneed the ribs of his steed and the beast stepped forward. "We're looking for the local witch. Have you seen her?"

Shang straightened. "Mistress Fen came here yesterday afternoon with medicine for my family. She left for the village shortly afterward. She said everyone had been stricken by the same disease as we were." He gestured at the household alter. "I thank the gods and my ancestors for sparing our family, but I would not recommend going into the village, sir."

"Your village chief said she came here," the bureaucrat spoke up.

Interesting that he said nothing about the plague flags I'd raised yesterday.

"That is concerning since she did not arrive here." Shang inclined his head. "I can send one of my sons to her dwelling to save such honored dignitaries a trip."

"If she's not here, then who's that?" The bureaucrat pointed at me.

"This is my new wife, Ling." Shang gestured for me to join him.

I kept my head lowered and shuffled forward as a proper wife would do. Hopefully, neither Po nor anyone else gave an accurate description of me to these men. I didn't have to fake my hands trembling inside my sleeves.

"I would have picked a younger wife," the bureaucrat sneered before he turned to Bao. From the corner my eye, I saw her as she shrank behind Xian. "And that one?"

"My daughter-in-law Bao," Shang replied.

"What is that delicious odor?" The sorcerer spoke for the first time.

Once again, Shang bowed. "Our family would be honored to host such august company for the evening meal."

Custom and honor worked in our favor. The soldiers dismounted, and the boys scurried to take the reins and lead their horses to the stream for a drink. They ignored Bao and me. While she fetched bowls and chopsticks, I reached into my pocket and sprinkled the cucumber seeds into the stew.

The bureaucrat, the sorcerer, and the captain claimed Shang's table. The remaining soldiers sat on the outside steps. Once all our guests were served their dinner, I nodded to Bao. She slipped into Shang and Xian's sleeping room where they would help her and the infant prince out through the window. Despite their initial protests, I didn't want them near here when the sorcerer realized what I'd done.

Our guests plowed through their bowls of millet and stew while I served the three inside the remainder of Shang's rice wine.

"Where's your husband?" the bureaucrat asked.

"Tending to your horses, sir."

"Then where's your daughter-in-law?" He laughed. "Maybe the two of you could be our entertainment."

He grabbed for me, but I evaded him. I wasn't sure how much longer I could keep up this charade. A breeze swept through the open windows.

Dragon magic.

The sweet sound I'd been waiting for came to my ears. Men wretching in the courtyard.

The captain stumbled to his feet, only to fall to his knees and vomit.

The bureaucrat pushed away from the table, his eyes wide. "You poisoned us!"

"I did not, sir." I smiled at the sorcerer. "Your compatriot did by killing our pigs."

"The pork," the sorcerer snarled. He threw his nearly empty bowl at my head, but his aim was ruined by his shaking. I dodged it easily.

A black and white body dropped from the rafter to land lightly on my shoulder. "And I would add, the Venerable Jin is not happy with your actions either. I suggest you remove the curse from him."

The assumption the dragon had given me his name should have given the sorcerer pause. Instead, he muttered something under his breath. His shaking stopped. "I'll destroy you first, witch."

And I had no doubt he would do exactly that if I allowed him the chance. My fingers sketched a word in the air, and I whispered, "Grow."

The sorcerer clutched his abdomen and screamed. He fell to the floor, writhing. Green tendrils sprouted from his nose and mouth. Between one breath and the next, flowers bloomed on the cucumber plants. More vines burst from his skin. His body stilled and disappeared beneath runners, leaves and tiny cucumbers.

The captain wiped his mouth with the back of his hand. "Would you mind explaining what just happened?"

I raised my hand, but he shook his head. "I'm not your enemy, Mistress Fen."

I glanced at the dragon, and his tail waved. If he trusted the captain, that was sufficient for me. I crossed my arms and glared at the bureaucrat. "You might want ask his co-conspirator."

"She lies!" the bureaucrat cried. "And she murdered Zhou. Arrest her, Hong!"

The dragon growled. Twin plumes of smoke rose from his nostrils along with a few embers. It was too much for the bureaucrat. He squealed and stumbled out of Shang's cottage.

"The first minister suspected their treachery. I was to arrest them once we recovered the prince. Don't worry. He won't get far." Captain Hong winked at me. His gesture was followed by shouts and a crash. We both winced.

He rose to his feet and peeked through a window. "Before we attend to the stone cutter's alter and clean his home, might I trouble you for a stomach remedy, Mistress Fen?"

A week later, we arrived at the imperial palace. And I prayed to all the gods that I never rode a horse again as I dismounted.

Jin draped himself about my shoulders. Every time the bureaucrats or soldiers tried to separate Shang and me, smoke poured from the dragon's nostrils. Every time some official asked, or demanded, to take the baby, the dragon hissed and snapped at them until they backed away.

Or he did until we were escorted before the emperor.

My attention was consumed by the immense dragon laying at the foot of the steps leading to the throne. Its scales shone gold and azure beneath the thousands of lamps. Eyes the color of sapphires and the size of plates regarded us. Her visage seemed downright friendly compared to the ugly scowls from the nobles and ladies of the court.

The woman seated next to the emperor cried out when she saw us. My heart wanted to jump out of my chest. The baby wasn't just any prince. He was the son of the emperor's first wife.

The heir to the Dragon Throne.

"Approach, child." The adult dragon's voice vibrated across the finely polished jade and marble floor and through the soles of my shoes.

Captain Hong elbowed my ribs, and I crossed what was to me an immense expanse and hesitated at the steps. My black and white companion scrambled down my clothing and skittered to his larger friend. They both looked at me and nodded.

The climb seemed to take an eternity. I wasn't foolish enough to climb to the top. I stopped two steps below the first wife and handed her son to her. She sobbed and clutched him tightly. I bowed deeply to the emperor.

"Thank you for your service to us, Mistress Fen."

I assumed it was the emperor who spoke. I didn't dare look to make sure. Keeping my head low, I backed down the steps.

When both of my feet landed on the polished floor, the larger dragon said, "Wait, child."

I froze, not sure what to expect next. What did she want from me? I dared a peek from beneath my eyelashes.

Her massive head turned toward the throne. "My son has claimed his name, and he has chosen Mistress Fen as his human."

A flurry of gasps rose around us.

"That's impossible!" The same male voice as before. Definitely the emperor. "I declared—"

"And who whispered that suggestion into your ear?" she purred. "We protect your empire at our pleasure, not yours. My son served above and beyond to save your heir when you disregarded my advice. His life is now his to do with as he wishes."

Silence reigned in the throne room.

"And while none of us can restore the lives claimed by Sorcerer Zhou's curse," the imperial dragon continued. "Mistress Fen and her village will be recompensed for their other losses."

"Captain Hong," the emperor's voice rang out. "You will see that Mistress Fen and her companion are supplied, and you will escort them home."

I prayed the dragons hadn't invited more disaster upon us. No emperor would take such a public chastisement lightly.

The little one scrambled up my clothing and perched on my shoulder once again. We backed out of the throne room and Hong led us outside. The captain ordered Shang and I to wait at a bench in the main courtyard while he arranged for wagons, replacement animals and goods.

I eyed the dragon. "Was this your plan all along?"

"No." His voice was high and sweet.

I tried to tamp down my annoyance, but I couldn't. "You could speak the whole time?"

"No, that was part of the curse."

"The curse was lifted a week ago," I snapped.

Shang rested a hand on my arm. "Fen . . ."

The dragon scrambled down to my lap and bowed. "Greetings, Mistress Fen. I am Jin, and I wish to serve as your protector."

Shang chuckled. "Jin, huh?"

"I like it." Jin's whiskers waved. "Daquan chose well."

I groaned. "Daquan will be at my place all the time thanks to you."

"Well . . ." Jin's gold eyes dropped. "If you and Shang were married, I would be your family's protector."

My jaw dropped.

Shang laughed loud and long. "Good luck with that plan."

Jin's tail waved lazily. "I'm a dragon. We're very patient, and we always get what we want."

Want some more witchy adventures? Turn the page for a special excerpt of the first book in the Millersburg Magick Mysteries, *Spells and Sleuths!*

Excerpt ©2021, Suzan Harden

Spells and Sleuths

When the dark cherry front door of Aunt Jo's coffee shop slammed open, Kirsten Wilson jumped. The coffee pot filled with the day's special, a fresh, hot Kona blend, slipped from her damp hand. She watched in slow-motion horror as the glass pot dropped toward the red and white tile floor.

Instinctively, she reached out with her powers. Unfortunately, her elemental specialty was water, not earth. The pot shattered against the ceramic tiles, but the java swirled and steamed in midair. Freezing wind blew through the doorway as Rose Gleason struggled to close the coffee shop door against the mid-morning autumn storm. Aunt Jo rushed over to help the elderly lady.

Kirsten grabbed a clean, empty pot. She concentrated a bit more and shifted the hot coffee from her bubble of magick into the new pot. Thank goodness, no other customers were in the shop. Even though the existence of supernaturals had been exposed due to their efforts to save the Normals who couldn't evacuate Puget Sound when Mount Rainier had erupted twelve years ago, there was still a lot of suspicion and fear among the Normal community.

Not to mention, Mom and Dad always said not to show off.

Rain splattered even harder against the coffee shop's huge plate glass windows. The edges of the forest green awning over the entrance and windows danced and rippled from the storm's gusts. A few people hurried into the courthouse across the road, but no one treaded the sidewalks on this side of Jackson Street in such a blustery, wet, cold morning.

"I'm so sorry, ladies." Miz Rose panted. "Darn wind." She turned seventy last month, and from the way her fingers curled, her arthritis was getting worse. Between that, the drop in temperatures, and the fierce wind, no wonder she lost her grip on the brass door handle.

"What can we get you, Miz Rose?" Kirsten dumped the broken glass into the trash and wiped her hands on her orange apron as Jo helped their only customer out of her coat. Rose Gleason had been their 4-H Club advisor when Kirsten and her twin Kaley joined. She insisted her club members call her "Rose" because "Mrs. Gleason" was her mother-in-law. Holmes County,

Ohio, was far too conservative not to have an honorific, so "Miz Rose" had stuck as her name forever.

"A cinnamon latte, please." A frown creased Miz Rose's face. "But I'm not here for just coffee."

"Tarot card reading? A little gossip?" Jo grinned. Even though both women were the same age, the life expectancy for witches was one hundred-thirty years. Jo could have passed as Kirsten's older sister with the right hairstyle, clothes, and makeup. No gray marred Jo's mahogany braid, the same mahogany both Mom and Kirsten had. Thank goddess, Jo didn't wear elastic-waist polyester pants, but sometimes, she said something incongruous with her physical appearance.

When Kirsten's twin Kaley teased Jo about being old enough to see the first moon landing live on TV, their great aunt said the Rainier Outing was the best thing that ever happened. Otherwise, she would have had to sell her coffee shop and move to another town by now to avoid the scrutiny of Normals. And she could stop dying gray streaks in her hair.

Miz Rose toddled to her left, checking the matching cherry tables and chairs past the service counter and leading to the restrooms. There was nothing on that side of the store but the framed paintings and photos by local artists that hung on the off white walls. Once Miz Rose made sure they were alone in the coffee shop, she shuffled to a table closest to the radiator.

Kirsten started the espresso brewing while she kept an eye on their visitor. Despite Miz Rose knowing about the supernaturals long before the Outing, she and folks who were Mom's age or older still had a problem talking about woo-woo stuff in public. And if Miz Rose checked for privacy, that's exactly what she wanted to talk about.

Their elderly customer turned back to Jo. "Actually, I think I have a ghost problem." An even deeper wrinkle appeared above Miz Rose's bright orange glasses that matched her Halloween sweater. She gestured for Jo to join her before she carefully lowered herself into the wooden chair.

This month's coffee shop seat covers featured black cats and pumpkins appliqued on cream broad cloth. Mary Levy made them in addition to working the early morning shift at the coffee shop. She was currently in the back of the shop putting together salads and sandwiches in preparation for lunch.

Kirsten never quite understood why the Amish community were more accepting of the supernaturals than the rest of the Normals in Millersburg. Maybe because they were used to being outsiders, too. Though in Mary's case, her great-great-aunt Anne had been a vampire until the cure for the disease had been discovered.

Jo took the chair beside Rose where she could keep an eye on the front door. "Sweetie—" She patted Rose's hand. "—I told you before. Your mom has passed on. She's not there."

"I don't think it's Mother." The elderly woman's

eyes glistened behind her thick lens. "I think it's Dick. Wouldn't his death count as unfinished business?"

The giant picture windows at the front of the store shivered from a harsh blast of wind. The perky scent of the espresso mixed with the warm spice of cinnamon, though neither completely blocked the sweet odor of fresh baked pastries in the well-lit glass case on the right side of the register and counter.

Kirsten listened intently to the women as she steamed the milk for Rose's latte. Rose's brother had been murdered by the Millersburg Monster before Kirsten and her twin Kaley had been born.

Except there wasn't really a monster. Just a trapped Native American water spirit forced to kill against its will. But the monster version sounded cooler, and one of the Normal farmers used the idea for his cornfield maze every year. The event drew so many people from Cleveland and Columbus it drove Sheriff Birkheimer a little crazy trying to find extra help for traffic control for the month of October.

"What makes you think it's Mister Dick?" Kirsten asked. "If he was still hanging around, wouldn't he have made himself known long before now?"

At Jo's pursed her lips and glare, Kirsten ducked her head and retrieved the can of whipped cream from the mini-refrigerator under the counter.

"Rose, maybe it's time to think about—" Jo started.

Kirsten rolled her eyes. Sometimes, her great-aunt wasn't the most subtle person on the face of the planet.

Miz Rose's explosion of temper would have been expected by anybody else who dared suggest she was too old to be living alone in a giant Victorian.

"I am not moving!" The elderly woman's frail body shook. "That house has been in my family for six generations! I am not leaving!"

Kirsten set the hot cup in front of Miz Rose. "What if I come over after the lunch rush?"

This time, both Miz Rose and Jo glared at her.

"Shouldn't you be in school?" Miz Rose said, patting her damp, iron-gray locks back in place.

"Teacher in-service day." Kirsten squared her shoulders and faced Jo. "I can check out Miz Rose's house. If there's nothing, it'll relieve your mind. And if there's something—"

"You'll come get me." Jo leaned back in her chair and crossed her arms. "The last thing we need is a ghost possessing you, young lady."

Oh, geez! Like she'd be stupid enough to let a ghost kick her out of her own body. But somehow, Kirsten squelched the urge to roll her eyes again. If she did, Jo would forbid her from going to Rose's house.

Right before Jo tattled on her to Mom.

"If there's something in Miz Rose's house, I'll come straight back here and let you know." Kirsten shut up and waited, a trick her twin never understood. She knew the I-just-turned-eighteen argument wouldn't fly with her great-aunt.

Finally, the crinkles around Jo's eyes eased, and her

nostrils flared as she exhaled. "Fine. But I want you to call me before you go home, and let me know either way."

"Yes, ma'am."

Jo inclined her head toward the kitchen. "Tell Mary to take it easy on the salads. A dozen will do." She turned to watch the street. A couple of minivans rolled by, but no pedestrians. Raindrops smacked the huge picture windows with sharp little reports. Jo shook her head. "I don't think we'll get much business with this weather."

Turned out, Jo was so very wrong on that count. Between the cold wind and spitting rain, half of Millersburg decided they wanted something hot, whether it be soup or coffee, to go with their salad or sandwich. In fact, it was nearly three before business died enough for Kirsten to clock out.

"You still going to Rose's house?" Jo eyed Kirsten.

"Yes, ma'am, I am," she answered as she slung on her burgundy waterproof jacket.

Jo inclined her head toward the back of the shop and lowered her voice. "There's some white sage sticks in my desk. Bottom drawer on the right."

"Thanks, Aunt Jo." Kirsten grinned and headed toward the storeroom cum office. Once she secured two of the sage sticks, a pack of matches, and a Ziploc bag of salt in a larger Ziploc to keep everything dry inside her backpack, she returned to the front to find Kaley leaning against the pastry display case. Her twin wore her varsity jacket and jeans.

Like cheerleaders should get to wear a varsity jacket.

"I don't get your fingerprints all over that," Kirsten snapped. "I just cleaned the glass."

"Be nice to me if you want a ride home in the rain," Kaley shot back, flipping her bottle-blond hair over her shoulder in the process. "Mom sent me to get you."

"Fine. But I have a stop first." Kirsten turned and waved. "See you Saturday morning, Jo!"

Their great-aunt waved absently before turning back to Augusta Wright who was ordering pastries for next week's Ladies Auxiliary meeting. Once they were outside, Kirsten could feel her sister's eyes on her despite them both ducking their heads against the wind and the rain.

"Where do we need to go?" Kaley yelled over the ropes slapping against the flagpole in front of the courthouse. "I've got some time before I need to be at Tina's."

Kirsten shook her head. "Babysitting again?"

Kaley shrugged. "After her ugly divorce, I don't blame her for wanting to go out for some stress relief."

Despite having a good job in the Pomerene Hospital administration department, Tina Eisler's idea of stress relief involved sleeping with every eligible male in Holmes County, plus a couple of ineligible ones. She really needed to pay more attention to her two kids, who were hurting just as bad as she was. However, Kirsten kept her mouth shut on that topic. Mom treated Tina like her little sister no matter how bad Tina screwed up at life or magick.

"What?" Kaley said as they rounded the shop and crossed the parking lot. "No smart ass comments about Tina?"

"Not today. I need to get over to the old Miller Mansion."

"Miz Rose's place? Why?"

"I just need to check out a problem she's having."

"What kind of problem?" Kaley tapped the key fob to unlock the doors of Mom's little sedan. When Kirsten remained silent after they climbed inside, Kaley waved the fob. "Spill unless you want to walk there in the rain."

Kirsten sighed. No, she didn't. It was only spitting rain now, but more gray clouds darkened the sky to the west. She wouldn't make to Miz Rose's house before the next wave hit.

On the other hand, she wanted to prove to both Mom and Jo she could handle things on her own. Kaley didn't take her magick studies as seriously, and their older relatives assumed her lack of focus applied to Kirsten as well. It irritated the hell out of her.

"Miz Rose thinks she has a ghost."

"Awesome!" Kaley flashed a maniacal grin before she

pressed the button to start the car. "I'm coming with you if you're going to bust a ghost."

"What about Tina's kids?"

"I don't have to be there until seven." Kaley back out of the spot. "Plenty of time."

Kirsten leaned back in the passenger seat. Part of her was annoyed by her sister tagging along. But another part was glad to have backup.

Just in case there really was a ghost haunting Miz Rose's house.

Acknowledgements

Thank you to editor extraordinaire Elisabeth Waters for taking a chance on a brand-new writer. And thank you to Jaye Manus for putting up with my tardiness when reviewing her beautiful designs.

Much love to Darling Husband, Genius Kid, and Significant Other. And we can't wait to meet Adorable Spawn this summer!

About the Author

Suzan Harden transitioned from writing information technology manuals for companies and legal articles for a law enforcement magazine to her first love, fantasy and science fiction in all their forms. She's the author of the Bloodlines, the 888-555-HERO, and the Justice series.

www.ingramcontent.com/pod-product-compliance
Lightning Source LLC
Chambersburg PA
CBHW071021180726
48291CB00004B/1568